THE BOY RECESSION

by FLYNN MEANEY

poppy

LITTLE, BROWN AND COMPANY
New York   Boston

Poppy

Hachette Book Group
237 Park Avenue, New York, NY 10017
For more of your favorite series, visit our website at www.pickapoppy.com

Poppy is an imprint of Little, Brown and Company.
The Poppy name and logo are trademarks of Hachette Book Group, Inc.

The publisher is not responsible for websites (or their content) that are not owned by the publisher.

First Edition: August 2012

Library of Congress Cataloging-in-Publication Data

Meaney, Flynn.
The boy recession / by Flynn Meaney. — 1st ed.
p. cm.
"Poppy."
Summary: When all the boys start transferring out of Julius P. Heil High, a lovable slacker becomes a hot commodity much to his best friend's bewilderment.
ISBN 978-0-316-10213-1
[1. High schools—Fiction. 2. Schools—Fiction. 3. Dating (Social customs)—Fiction. 4. Wisconsin—Fiction.] I. Title.
PZ7.M5118Bo 2012
[Fic]—dc23
2011027354

10 9 8 7 6 5 4 3 2 1

RRD-C

Printed in the United States of America

Book design by Saho Fujii

Also by Flynn Meaney

Bloodthirsty

For my gal pals,
and the nights we spent scheming at Starbucks

CHAPTER 1: HUNTER

"Summer Jobs with Sex Appeal:
A Teen's Guide to Working in Whitefish Bay"

Aviva Roth for *The Julius Journal*,
Special Summer Break Edition

W hen are you gonna get off your lazy ass and get a job?"
Eugene asks me.

I'm so Zen right now, I don't even realize the kid is
talking to me. Eugene and Derek and I are out on Eugene's
sailboat on Lake Michigan. We're pretty close to shore
still, so the wind isn't too crazy here. It's just this nice
breeze rocking the boat a little bit back and forth as I lie
stretched out on the deck, the warmth of the sun on me.
Man, this is a nice day.

We live in Wisconsin, and in Wisconsin, you really
appreciate days when it's warm and sunny. In winter this
town is freezing. You step out your door in the morning
and the whole place looks like one of those nature specials
in which a guy brings a camcorder to the North Pole and
then the camera cuts out and you hear on the news that he

got eaten by a bear. Since school starts next week, I'm taking advantage of the last full day I have to lie on my ass and do nothing.

"Hunter!" Eugene says. "Are you gonna get your act together for the school year or what? You were supposed to get a summer job, and the summer's over."

"I tried to get a summer job," I tell Eugene, sitting up and yawning.

I open my eyes, but the sun is really bright, because I've been lying down with my arm over my face for so long.

"It's, like, a recession, dude."

It's Eugene's sailboat, and he's doing something sailboaty—tying a knot, or something like that. Like usual, he's dressed like an eighty-year-old dude on a golf course— pink shirt and shoes with tassels and all that crap. Even though he's wearing big sunglasses, I can tell he's rolling his eyes.

"It's a recession, for real!" I tell him, lifting up my T-shirt to scratch my stomach. "My dad hasn't had a job for, like, six months."

Derek's sitting balanced on the side of the boat. He thinks he's a badass for balancing there, but the boat is barely moving at all, so he's definitely not gonna fall off. Derek actually came out here to fish, but we're so close to the docks and the beach and the people swimming there that he's not catching anything. Now he puts down his fishing pole and swings his legs around so he's facing us.

"I thought your dad was a stay-at-home dad, Huntro," Derek says.

Derek and Eugene call me "Huntro" sometimes. I have no clue why.

"He's not a stay-at-home dad," I scoff. "He has one kid, and it's me. If he's supposed to be watching me, or whatever, full-time, he's doing a crappy job. Because I'm out every night, doing stupid shit with you guys."

"Don't be sexist, Huntro," Derek says. "Dudes can be stay-at-home dads, too. I think it would be pretty cool. I'd be one."

Derek's totally given up on fishing. He reaches into his pocket for a pack of Marlboros and shakes out one really old, wrinkly cigarette. I'm pretty sure he's had this same pack since eighth grade, when health class sparked his interest in smoking. He takes out a match, too, and strikes it on the brim of his hat.

"Yeah, you'd be a great role model," I tell him, lying back down on the boat deck.

Eugene is still all stressed out about my job search.

"Where did you apply this summer?" he asks me. "Did you actually apply for any jobs?"

"I did!" I say, putting my arm back over my eyes to block the sun. Whoa, I don't smell so good right now. I must be sweating through my shirt.

"I applied at the pool," I tell him. "To be, like, the snack-bar guy, or lifeguard, or something."

"Which one?" Eugene asks.

"I don't know. Maybe it was a job application for the lifeguard, and I wrote about snack-bar stuff."

Eugene sighs loudly. "What else?"

"Uh...I applied at Culver's, too. I was there, eating a bunch of Butter Burgers, and I saw a job application, so I grabbed it."

"So what about that?" Eugene says.

"Still waiting to hear back," I tell him. "Apparently, no one's impressed with my eating experience."

Man, I could really go for a Butter Burger right now.

"Hunter, you can't just sit around waiting for people to call you back," Eugene tells me. He stands up and starts to pace the deck.

"Finding a job is about bothering people. You've got to go door to door, ringing doorbells, finding old ladies who need you to do stuff to their chimneys. You gotta be willing to do anything. Go out and *find* something. You've got to get *aggressive*."

"I don't know," I say, yawning so wide I kind of drool on myself by accident. "I'm not a super-aggressive person."

"You're *Hunter*," Eugene tells me. "Be a *hunter*, Hunter."

It is pretty ironic that my name is Hunter. I'm actually much more of a gatherer. I don't do stuff; I let stuff happen to me. If we were still cavemen, I wouldn't be out there at dawn, stalking down buffalo and turning their bladders into beer mugs or whatever. I'm pretty sure I'd be sleeping in until someone dragged my ass out of that cave. And if I was hungry, I'd end up eating grass or ants or whatever you could scrounge up in the *Homo erectus* version of a vending machine.

Derek's still leaning on the side of the boat, but he's not smoking. He just keeps lighting matches against his hat and then holding them between two fingers, letting them burn down until they're close to his skin. Once they burn down, he throws them over the side of the boat, into the water.

"If you wanna help the kid out," Derek says to Eugene, "why don't *you* hire him?"

Actually, Eugene probably could hire me, since he's an "entrepreneur." That's what he calls himself. He makes most of his money buying beer for people's parties. Eugene's got a fake ID, and he actually gets away with using it because he looks like he's thirty-six, thanks to his devotion to tasseled shoes and his ridiculous carpet of chest hair. Besides buying beer, Eugene sells *Maxim* magazines and cigarettes, and does stuff like make fake notes so people can watch that *Miracle of Life* video in bio class. That's part of the reason he has this boat — he stores a lot of illegal shit on here.

"I don't think so," Eugene says. "No offense, Huntro, but I work in a high-pressure, high-stakes environment. I just can't take a chance on you."

I'm not offended. And I don't give a crap. I don't want to work for Eugene. Actually, I don't want to work at all. It will be hard enough to go back to school next week; I don't want a job on top of that. I've gotten way too used to my summer schedule: waking up at 2 PM, going to the pool, falling asleep in the sun without sunscreen, going home, going to Derek's house to wrestle in his wrestling ring (which is actually a bunch of mattresses in his basement), going home again to play *World of Warcraft* until 3 AM, then going to sleep after a day of being generally irresponsible.

"Ugh. Will you look at those douchebags?" Derek says. "Those preppy d-bags piss me off."

Derek is glaring over at the docks at a bunch of guys we go to school with, the guys who are really into school and sports and crap. These guys are on the student senate, go to dances, and throw keggers — and all the rest of that Zac Efron typical high-school crap. Right now, a bunch of them wearing plaid shorts are doing cannonballs off the dock.

Our town is Whitefish Bay, but people call it "White Folks Bay" because it's so preppy and privileged and whatever. A lot of the terrible stuff people say about the suburbs is true about Whitefish Bay. There are rich white kids who drink too much. There are spoiled kids who get Bimmers for their sixteenth birthdays, crash them, and then have their parents buy them new ones. This kinda stuff offends Derek; I don't let it get to me.

"Just ignore them," I tell Derek. "Let them have their fun with their plaid shorts. Don't be jealous."

"They're probably jealous of *us*," Eugene says, letting the mainsail out by unhooking a rope. "We've got a boat."

"Yeah, I'm sure," Derek says sarcastically. "We've got a boat, and they've got *girls*."

That's true. They do have girls. There are about thirty girls over on the dock with those plaid-shorts guys, and all those girls are wearing bikinis. Those guys have girls jumping on their backs, girls diving into the water with them, girls dunking their heads underwater, girls racing them back to the docks all soaking wet and hot. Eugene, Derek, and I don't have any girls. We never have any girls.

"Look at that crap," Derek says bitterly. "Look at those pricks with their abs and their...haircuts. Guys like that try to look all clean and shit so no one realizes how sketchy they are. Girls might think *we're* sketchy, but those guys are sketchy. Those guys are sexual assaults waiting to happen. Those are the guys who get girls wasted and take advantage of them."

Derek shakes his head and sits down on the deck next to me. He lights another match against his hat. Derek's kind of a pyromaniac — in case you haven't noticed. On the Fourth of July he had this whole plan; he was gonna learn how to become a fire-eater by watching YouTube videos. It didn't pan out, though, because his mom found out, and she stopped him because Derek's already been to the emergency room three times this year. So I guess he's pissed because that plan didn't pan out.

"Yeah, those guys get girls wasted on alcohol they buy from *me*," Eugene says. "Don't talk shit about my clients."

"Don't you ever get mad when you buy all their beer and deliver all their kegs and you don't even get invited to their parties?" Derek asks Eugene now.

Eugene shakes his head. "I just sit back and count up my money."

Now Eugene does that. He sits down in what he calls the "captain's chair," and he whips out his wallet. This kid carries an amazing amount of cash on him. Sometimes I think about pickpocketing him. It would be pretty easy—he's only, like, five-foot-three. I'm pretty sure I could rob him, no problem. Right now, though, I'm too lazy.

Derek's so busy glaring at a guy in plaid shorts who's groping this freshman girl underwater that he lets the match burn all the way down to his fingers.

"Shit!" he cries out, shaking the match so hard it drops to the floor of the boat.

Eugene looks up from his money, all pissed.

"Do *not* light my boat on fire," Eugene tells Derek.

"A boat can't catch on fire," Derek says. "If it does, we'll put it out. We've got *water* all around us."

He picks the match up off the boat deck and throws it over the side. He stays standing up and shades his eyes so he can watch the dock some more.

"You know who I want to punch in the face?" Derek says, stretching his arms over his head. "Charlie Devine."

When I sit up, my hair is all over my face. What I really want to do right now is jump in this water. I'm sweaty as balls.

"Don't you hate guys like that?" Derek asks me. "I seriously can't deal with those guys for another year."

"I don't really give a crap," I tell him. "I mean, yeah, girls like them better than us, so that sucks. And they have parties and we're not invited, but...whatever. I mean, we do stuff. And they're not invited to our stuff."

Derek rolls his eyes. "We hang out at the gas station and TP people's houses."

"And they're not invited!" I tell him, laughing.

"You know what girls call those pricks?" Derek says. "*The guys.* That's what they call them. They'll be planning their parties and crap, and they'll be like, 'What time are *the guys* getting here?' You know what that means, Huntro? They don't even count us. We're not even *guys* to them."

To be honest with ya, I don't like "the guys" any more than Derek does. But I don't get worked up about them. I'm not an angry dude. It's too much effort to get pissed off. The other night we were wrestling in Derek's basement and he accidentally crotch-stomped me. I didn't even get mad; I just forgot about it and ate some Fritos.

"You know what you need?" I tell Derek, throwing my arm around his shoulders.

He's blowing on the fingers he burned. "What?"

"A swim," I tell him.

Now I wrap both of my arms around him and start pushing him toward the boat railing. I think I can throw Derek overboard. I mean, he's stronger than Eugene, but I caught him by surprise, so I've got the advantage. Unless he lights me on fire, I'm gonna push him into that water.

CHAPTER 2: KELLY

"Summer Lovin':
Tips for Trapping Your Own Danny Zuko"

Aviva Roth for *The Julius Journal,*
Special Summer Break Edition

Do you ever feel bad our lives aren't more like *Grease*?" I ask Darcy.

It's the last day of summer vacation; Darcy, Aviva, and I are at the beach; and for the sixteenth year of my life, I'm disappointed with my tan. You can't even call this a tan. There's one strip of pinkish sunburned skin between the bottom of my tankini top and the top of my tankini bottom. That's it. That's as tan as I'm going to get this summer. In Wisconsin, we don't see the sun from October to April, so in a few months, I'll be able to go skiing naked and just blend in with the mountains.

I reach for Aviva's tanning oil to rub on my shoulders, but then I think, *What's the point?* and throw the bottle at Darcy, who hasn't answered my question. She's too busy reading this huge book that's almost as big as her entire body. When I first met Darcy, I was seven years old and I was jealous of her blond hair and blue eyes because I thought she was like Tinker Bell. I found out pretty quickly that she is nothing like Tinker Bell. I don't think Tinker Bell would be reading a book called *Shostakovich and Stalin.*

"Darcy!" I say.

When she gets to the end of the page, Darcy takes her blue zinc oxide–covered nose out of the book and repeats, "Do I ever feel bad our lives aren't more like *Grease?*"

"Uh-huh," I say.

I spray some Sun-In in my hair. As well as being my last chance for a tan, today is my last chance for natural highlights. And by "natural," I mean highlights made by spraying my hair with sticky fake-lemon-scented spray and then sitting in the sun, crossing my fingers that all those reports of the ozone layer breakdown are true. Maybe if I go back to school tomorrow all tan and blond, people will think I went to some exotic island this summer.

Darcy holds her place in her book with her finger and asks for clarification.

"You mean like ancient, naked-Olympics Greece, or economically corrupt modern-day Greece?"

I snatch Darcy's huge book out of her hands and put it on Aviva's towel, which is on the other side of mine.

"You need to stop reading at the beach," I tell her. "School starts tomorrow. This is our last day to gossip and have fun."

"That is fun!" Darcy whines. "That's my fun book!"

"Why would I want our lives to be like economically corrupt modern-day Greece?" I ask. "I'm talking about *Grease Grease.*"

I grab Aviva's pink iPod off her towel and scroll through the summer playlist I made for her. I choose "Summer Nights," which I put on the list after my seven-year-old sister, Lila, made me watch *Grease* five times in one week, and put the volume up so Darcy can hear the opening notes.

"Oh, the movie *Grease,*" Darcy says. She's obviously disappointed I'm not trying to start a conversation about gross domestic product. "The movie *Grease*? No way. Drag racing and pregnancy scares? I don't think so, Kell."

"But it's so cute on the first day of school, when Sandy's telling everyone about her and Danny, and how they met on the beach, and they were so cute together, drinking lemonade. I didn't do any of that stuff this summer. We're sixteen. Shouldn't we be summer loving?"

Darcy is slathering her arms in SPF 85. At least I look tan compared to her. She could fly to Canada right now and ski naked—not that she would ever be naked in public.

"It looks like Aviva's getting some summer loving," she says, shading her eyes and looking out at Lake Michigan.

My other best friend, Aviva, is with a cute lifeguard on the dock. She just jumped on his back and wrapped her ridiculously long legs around him. The lifeguard is jogging down the dock, and when he jumps off the end, Aviva is still on his back. After a minute underwater, she pops her head up above water and laughs in the guy's face. When she climbs back up onto the dock, Darcy and I can see down her bikini top from fifty yards away. According to Aviva, it was her good karma that gave her boobs that look amazing in a bikini top that doesn't even have underwire in it.

She also says that people stare at her a lot because she's one of the three and a half black people in Whitefish Bay—she's actually the half, because her mom is black and her dad is white. But it's actually because she's really pretty. And because she decided to have a "braless summer." Now she gets stared at the most often in places with air-conditioning.

"That's not summer love," I tell Darcy. "Aviva's gonna do what Aviva always does. Make out with him, then defriend him on Facebook and move on to someone else."

Darcy, Aviva, and I have been best friends since fourth grade, when we were in the advanced reading group together. Aviva gives me credit for holding the three of us together. I'm a Libra, which is all about balance, and Aviva claims I balance her and Darcy out with my normalcy. I guess you could look at it that way. Like, Aviva has those amazing boobs, Darcy has no boobs, and I can go either way, depending on how much effort and how many Victoria's Secret products are involved. Right now, Darcy's wearing a one-piece bathing suit that the Pope would approve of, I'm wearing a tankini that shows only the decent part of my stomach, and, out on the dock, Aviva's bikini bottom is creeping toward thong status.

It's the same thing with boys. Aviva is interested in a different boy every day. Darcy won't let herself get interested in any boy. (Except Stalin. And maybe Shostakovich.) Me, I just want one normal, nice boy to crush on.

But the thing about being normal is no one notices you. I blend in. I always have. In my fourth-grade school picture, I was in the middle row with a bunch of other girls with long brown hair, bangs, and headbands. My mom pointed to the picture and said, "You look so cute!"

She was pointing to Maddy Berg, another girl in my class.

Blending in wouldn't bother me, except I think it's contributing to the patheticness of my pathetic love life. I've never had any summer lovin'. And I've never had any school year lovin', either. I've never had a boyfriend. I've never hooked up with a guy. And this morning, on my Internet browser, an article popped up about women marrying themselves.

Even my wireless connection knows I'm alone.

I've been semi-depressed all day, realizing another summer has gone by without me having a boyfriend or even a crush. I'm picturing myself buying my own prom corsage, ordering a giant cake with three layers, and showing up at a scientific lab and asking if they've perfected asexual reproduction yet.

My sad daydreams are interrupted by Aviva, who

comes back from the lake dripping wet and shakes out her towel, getting water and sand all over me.

"How's what's-his-face?" I ask Aviva.

"He won't last long," she says, tilting her head and rubbing her towel against her ear.

"You're sick of him already?" Darcy asks.

"No," Aviva says darkly. "He has a very suspicious mole on his shoulder."

Darcy turns to me and rolls her eyes.

Aviva cheers up quickly and says, "I burned off a lot of calories flirting. Can we go get frozen custard?"

"No way." Darcy shakes her head. "That's so unhealthy. I brought snacks!"

It's not a real trip to the beach unless Darcy brings three books, SPF 85, and a mini-cooler — which she opens now, to take out a box of blueberries.

"They have antioxidants!" she says. "They keep your skin young."

"Young?" Aviva makes a face. "What do I want with that? Darce, stop with the sunscreen and the antioxidants. We already look young. Find me a berry that makes me look twenty-one. Find me a berry that will get me into an R-rated movie."

Darcy's about to lecture her, but I interrupt to keep peace.

"Darce, you eat the blueberries," I tell her. "The ice-cream truck is here. I'm gonna get Viva and me snacks that will make us old and fat."

"Ooh, Choco Tacos!" Aviva says, stretching out full-length on her towel, with sand clinging all over her wet body. "Those will do the trick!"

"Hey, Kelly!"

As I walk toward the ice-cream truck, shaking sand on the sidewalk with my flip-flops, Hunter Fahrenbach comes at me on his skateboard. Hunter and I are friends and have been in the school band together since freshman year. Darcy calls him Hairface Hunter, because his hair goes down past his chin—and it's usually hanging in his face. Right now, it's soaking wet. Actually, all of him is soaking wet—his shirt, his khaki shorts, his socks. His sneakers make squishing sounds as he stops short in front of me and gets off his skateboard.

"I would hug you, but..." Hunter holds out his arms, displaying his wet shirt, and grins.

"What happened to you?" I ask him, laughing.

"I jumped off Eugene's boat. With all my clothes on... obviously."

Hunter and I talk a lot during band, but we don't hang out much outside of class. I guess it's because he's busy doing crazy things like hanging around the gas station and setting stuff on fire. And, apparently, jumping into Lake Michigan fully clothed.

"What did you do this summer?" I ask him, adjusting the tankini strap because it's rubbing against my sunburn.

"Just hung out so far," Hunter says, putting one foot up on his skateboard and rolling it back and forth. "I'm supposed to find a summer job, but I haven't gotten around to it yet."

"Um, you know school starts tomorrow, right?" I ask him, smiling.

"Oh, crap, right," Hunter says, looking up at me from under his hair. He breaks out smiling when he sees me smiling. "I guess I can stop job hunting, then!"

He takes his foot off his skateboard and asks, "What have you been up to?"

"I worked at a music camp," I tell him. "I taught the cutest little kids."

"Oh, yeah?" Hunter says. "The Lieutenant will be happy with you."

I laugh. The Lieutenant is our band teacher, who was in the Marines for ten years. She makes us call her Lieutenant, and also makes us play patriotic music at every single concert. My dad refuses to videotape our performances anymore, because he's so sick of the "Armed Forces Medley."

"Oh, guess what I heard?" I say. "We're getting a piccolo! A freshman is coming in."

"No way!" Hunter says. "The Lieutenant is always saying we need a piccolo. What's that song she wants to play that has a big piccolo part?"

"'Stars and Stripes Forever,'" I say. "I know, she's always talking about that song! But get this. This is the best part. It's a guy!"

"The piccolo?" Hunter says. He's so surprised he lets his skateboard roll away from him, and he has to jog a few steps to stop it with his foot. "We're getting a *guy* piccolo?"

I'm sure there's a male piccolo player in every orchestra in the world. But the piccolo is such a tiny, squeaky little leprechaun instrument that it seems like something a high-school guy would get beat up for playing.

Hunter must be thinking the same thing, because he says, "That kid's got to have balls to play that weird little thing in public."

Hunter sounds so...impressed...that I have to laugh.

"Should be an interesting year," he says. "I gotta take off. I'll see ya tomorrow, though. Bye, dude."

"Bye...dude," I say as he skates away.

I head for the ice-cream truck, and my bad mood returns. Maybe it will be an interesting year for Hunter or an interesting year in band. But I doubt it will be an interesting year for me. It's hard to have an interesting year when you're the kind of girl that guys call "dude."

CHAPTER 3: KELLY

"Popularity of Plaid Shorts Plummets
as Preppies Flee Julius"

Aviva Roth for *The Julius Journal*, September

Happy First Day of School!" Darcy chimes when I get into her car.

Before I can sit in her passenger seat, I have to move Darcy's huge backpack that's full of a month's worth of books. Then I have to buckle my seat belt, because Darcy won't even shift out of park until I'm buckled.

"What are you so happy about?" I ask her irritably.

I'm pulling on the right side of my hair, which is wet. The left side is dry. Last year I had way too many messy-bun days, so I made this resolution that I was going to blow-dry my hair every morning of junior year. But today I had time to blow-dry only one side of it before Darcy was honking outside my house. On the first day of school, Darcy drives both Aviva and me so she can force us to be on time. Every other day, Aviva drives me, and Darcy arrives freakishly early on her own.

"All the boys are gone!" Darcy announces.

"What? What boys?"

I wish I could tilt Darcy's side-view mirror so I could see the right side of my head, but she would freak out. She has very strict rules about the angles of her mirrors.

"All the boys!" Darcy says. "All the Devine brothers transferred out of our school. And all the McKennas."

There are four Devine brothers, all of whom are really smart and cute and preppy. Charlie Devine, the oldest one, is president of our student senate. And there are five McKenna brothers, all of whom are amazing athletes—and also really cute. Mrs. Devine and Mrs. McKenna are really competitive with each other. They fight over everything. They end up taking up three pages of ads in the back of the yearbook every year, because they try to one-up each other by buying more space. Mrs. Devine is always bragging about Charlie's grades, because she's still angry that Mrs. McKenna beat her by having that fifth son. The girls of Julius P. Heil High School are really grateful for this rivalry, because, besides being entertaining at school fairs, it's produced so many beautiful boys for us to look at.

"Why did they leave?" I ask. "How could they leave? They're involved with so much stuff! Pierce McKenna is the whole reason our football team is good!"

"Remember the budget cuts I told you about? How teachers were leaving because Julius did a salary freeze?"

"Um, sure," I say.

I didn't understand everything Darcy told me about the salary negotiations she sat in on as student senate rep. But she did report back that one teacher dropped the F-bomb when talking to our principal—although she wouldn't tell us which teacher it was.

"So the football coach left for this prep school in Milwaukee," Darcy says. "And Pierce McKenna followed him, so he can get his college football scholarship or whatever. All the McKennas are going to prep school now, so once Mrs. Devine found out, she found a *better* prep school in Chicago, and the Devines are going there. They said it was because Mr. McDonnell left, and Charlie needed a good guidance counselor to get into Georgetown."

"You're not worried that Mr. McDonnell left?" I ask Darcy as she turns onto Aviva's street.

Mr. McDonnell was the guidance counselor for all the really uptight kids who started taking practice SATs in the seventh grade—i.e., Darcy. Lots of Mr. McDonnell's kids joined the band last year after there was an article in the *Tribune* saying playing the oboe could get you into college.

"Please," Darcy scoffs. "I've had my college essays written for eighteen months now."

She stops in front of Aviva's house—the biggest of any of our houses, which is unfair, because Aviva is an only child—and honks really loudly.

"But Charlie Devine is the president of our school," I remind her.

When Darcy turns to me, she's grinning like a maniac. She shakes her head.

"Not anymore," she says.

Wait. Darcy is the vice president of the student senate. And once I caught her in the school computer lab researching presidential assassinations. She said it was for a report on John F. Kennedy, but I secretly wondered if she wanted Charlie out of the way so she could take over. No wonder she's so happy. With Charlie gone, Darcy takes over as...

"I'm the president of the United States!" Darcy bursts out, unable to hold her announcement any longer. "I mean, of Julius P. Heil High School."

"Okay, let's not get ahead of ourselves," I caution her.

Great. Darcy is the ruler of our school. Pretty soon, Julius is going to be like Singapore — you'll get a $500 fine for chewing gum or making out in the hallways. *Oh, well.* The making-out thing won't affect me. And the boys leaving won't affect me, either. My love life couldn't be more nonexistent if Julius was an all-girls' boarding school with a moat full of alligators around it. I give up on pulling on the wet side of my hair and let it go frizzy as we wait for Aviva.

Now, I am not a morning person, but Aviva takes not being a morning person to the extreme. Every time we pick her up, she stumbles out of her house like she's hungover — or still drunk — from some party the night before. It's not true, because Aviva doesn't drink, but that's how she looks. Today she comes stumbling out of her house in a loose black off-the-shoulder top and short black shorts and immediately winces at the sun in her eyes. She fishes her big black sunglasses out of her messenger bag, puts them on, and starts clomping across her wet lawn in four-inch wedges, walking right through the spray of a rotating sprinkler.

Darcy rolls down her window and says, "Dry yourself off before you get in my car!"

Aviva makes some vague attempt to wipe her wet legs with her wet hands, and then gets in the backseat and curls up in the fetal position, moaning.

"Morning, sunshine," I say, looking back at her and grinning. "I see black is the new black?"

"I'm in mourning!" Aviva declares dramatically.

"You still have to buckle your seat belt," Darcy says, waiting patiently to shift into drive.

"What are you mourning?" I ask Aviva, watching her buckle.

"All the boys are gone!" she whines. "Pierce McKenna left, so the other guys who wanted football scholarships left, too! All the boys are gone!"

"Well, not *all* of them," I say. Then I get nervous. "Right?"

As Darcy pulls away from her house, Aviva starts to count on her fingers.

"All of the Devines. That's four. All of the McKennas,

which makes nine. And then *six* other guys from the foot-ball team!"

Aviva throws up her hands in despair. She ran out of fingers.

"Fifteen boys," she says. "Fifteen boys, and we go to the tiniest school of all time. That's, like, sixty percent of the male population."

Darcy raises her eyebrows right away at that dubious calculation. Without taking her eyes off the road for a sec-ond, she corrects Aviva.

"There are approximately two hundred fifty students at Julius P. Heil High School, so we'll say for argument's sake that one hundred twenty-five of them are male. If fif-teen of those one hundred twenty-five left, that's only twelve percent of the male population. *Not* sixty."

"Aha!" Aviva says, leaning forward to stick her head between our seats. "Twelve percent of the *population*. But sixty percent of the *hotness*."

"You shouldn't care, anyway," I tell her. "You already made out with most of the guys at Julius. You hooked up with two Devines and the three cutest McKennas."

"Yeah, but some of them I kissed before puberty," Aviva says. "I was gonna give them a second go-around now that they have facial hair."

"I'm sure you'll find someone," I tell her. "You always do. You can reignite your imaginary relationship with that cute teacher's assistant."

"He probably left, too," Aviva says. "There's a complete

exodus of testosterone. I don't know what I did to deserve this. Where is this horrible boy karma coming from?"

"Maybe it's because you always make out with boys and then refuse to talk to them," I tell her.

"Do they not like that?" she asks. Then she sighs and asks Darcy, "Can we go to Starbucks? I need an iced mocha to cheer me up."

"No! We're turning into school right now!" Darcy says. "I have to get there early to sit in on the budget-cuts meeting with Dr. Nicholas before first period."

Dr. Nicholas is our principal, who everyone calls "Dr. Nicotine" because every year he tries and fails to quit smoking. I'm guessing if he has to deal with budget cuts, this will be another year he fails.

"What budget cuts?" I ask her. "Is there other stuff besides the teachers leaving?"

"Just frivolous stuff," Darcy says. "Like sports and the arts."

"The arts?" I ask her. "What about the arts?"

"I don't know yet. I'll find out in my meeting and tell you after," Darcy says. "But don't worry, Kell. I'll fight against anything that screws us over."

I want to ask about band, but Darcy's making a big show of pulling into the best space in the parking lot — the first front-row spot, the closest one to the school building. This is the school president's spot.

"Crap," Aviva says as she takes off her seat belt. "This reminds me — I forgot to enter the parking raffle!"

The parking raffle decides who gets the good spots in the Julius parking lot—the VIP parking. These spots are mostly taken up by senior and junior girls we call "spandexers" because they always wear thongs and tight stretchy pants to school. These girls are so devoted to showing off their asses that they join the volleyball, field hockey, and tennis teams just so they can spend more time wearing spandex. Darcy, Aviva, and I dislike most of them. I would say they're our enemies, but it's pretty hard to have enemies when your entire class has sixty-five people in it. You keep bumping into them and being assigned group projects with them, and you figure out how to get along.

Unless you're Aviva, and you're in a bad mood because boy karma is biting you in the ass.

"Ugh, look at this place," she says as she gets out of the car and sees a group of spandexers smoking and drinking coffee in an empty parking space. There's not a boy in sight.

"There's so many *girls*," Aviva says in disgust. "Yuck."

It turns out that one of the "frivolous" changes Darcy mentioned was that Julius got rid of the school band. Dr. Nicotine let the Lieutenant go. My first reaction when I heard was to wonder if the Lieutenant was the one who dropped that F-bomb. My second was to feel really bad for her. I hope she found another job, and that some school in Iowa is playing the "Armed Forces Medley" for the first time and is actually excited about it.

After her meeting, Darcy came and found me and promised me she would lobby the school board to get band back. But for now, I'm supposed to sign up for a study hall. I don't. Instead of going to the guidance office to change my schedule like all the other band kids do, I go to the band room, just like I have every third period since freshman year.

The room is so depressingly...neat. The chairs on the bandstand are in perfect rows. The music stands are all the same height. This is how the Lieutenant always wanted the room to look, and now she's not here to see it. Personally, I liked the messy chaos when there were fifty people in here—everyone tripping over the open euphonium cases, the clarinets passing around sheet music one of them forgot, the tubas emptying their spit valves onto the bandstand...okay, that last one was not sexy. Maybe I won't miss that.

My favorite thing in the band room is still here, though: the large-scale score of "Rhapsody in Blue" that's painted on the wall. It must have been painted there before the Lieutenant, because "Rhapsody in Blue" has nothing to do with the military or the American flag. It's a jazz-classical Gershwin song.

I love it, mostly because of the first time I played it, in this room. In third grade, we were bused here from the elementary school twice a week for beginner band. There were about fifteen of us learning the flute, but I was the first one to actually make a sound, and the first one to read music. So the Lieutenant let me read "Rhapsody in Blue" and play it right off the wall. Everyone else watched, and when I was done, they clapped.

Now I walk over, climb up onto the director's chair, which is against the "Rhapsody in Blue" wall, and trace the blue-paint notes with my finger. Then I swing around so I'm facing the bandstand and see that the baton is still on the director's music stand. I lift it and begin to direct the rows of empty chairs.

Then the door opens. *Uh-oh.* I drop the baton, and it bounces against the music stand before rolling onto the floor. I'm pretty sure I shouldn't be in this room right now, and I hope it isn't a teacher at the door.

But it's not—it's Hunter. He opens one of the practice-room doors.

"Hunter?"

Hunter stops short, then comes toward me, laughing.

"Oh, crap," Hunter says, laughing. "You scared me! I feel like this is forbidden territory now, or something."

"I know," I say. "I guess it is. No more band."

"I didn't think Julius could be any more cheap," Hunter says. "They're still using Office 95 in the computer labs."

"Do you think Dr. Nicholas sold the practice instruments on eBay?" I ask him, pointing to the empty cubbies.

Hunter steps back, looking at the cubbies.

"Whoa!" he says. "I didn't even notice that. Man, this sucks. This was my only extracurricular."

Hunter hops up onto the grand piano, which is covered in a black quilted cover, and swings his legs, kicking the bench with his untied Chuck Taylors.

"Do you remember beginner band?" I ask Hunter. "In third grade? They won't have it for the third-graders now."

"Yeah, that was when I played the drums for the first time," Hunter says. "I think it was good for me. It really mellowed me out."

"It was good! We need stuff like that!" I say. "They can't cut arts programs. This isn't some Disney Channel movie where the Jonas Brothers throw a benefit concert at the end to save the day."

Hunter laughs.

"Ya know, my mom works at another high school," he says, "where the seniors teach the freshmen music. It's called peer music...something."

"Peer music something?" I say. "Is that PMS for short?" We both laugh, then I say, "That's actually a good idea, though. We should have something like that!"

"We should definitely have PMS."

"I bet that would work!"

"I dunno." Hunter shrugs. "I'm not sure if it actually works. I think the school just can't afford real teachers."

"We can't afford real teachers!"

Then the door opens again, and Hunter and I have a

moment of mutual panic. He puts his finger to his mouth, slides down from the piano, crouches on the floor, and lifts up the black piano cover, motioning to the space underneath. I climb down from the director's chair, glancing over behind the bandstand, and then crawl under the piano. Hunter follows me.

Turning my head back toward him, I half mouth, half whisper, "How did you think of this?"

"I get in trouble a lot," Hunter whispers.

I start to laugh but bring my hand to my mouth to keep quiet. Hunter reaches around me and carefully lifts the front of the piano cover so we can see who just walked in. It turns out we're squeezed under this piano for no reason; it's not a teacher. It's a boy who looks really young—I guess he's a freshman, because I've never seen him before. He's kind of cute, actually, in this interesting way. He has dark curly hair, and he's wearing khakis, a sweater—and clogs. Are guys supposed to wear clogs? Is anyone who's not a dancer in the Appalachian Mountains supposed to wear clogs? He's nice-looking, though, even with the clogs, and...is that a man purse? Or a pencil case? Or...

"The piccolo!"

I say it out loud without meaning to, and Hunter, with his shoulders shaking, puts his finger to his mouth. There's no teacher in here, and we don't have to worry about getting caught, so we shouldn't be under the piano, but now we have to worry about getting caught under the piano.

As we watch, the boy comes up close to the piano, looks

up at "Rhapsody in Blue" for a minute, sighs, and walks away, the little piccolo case swinging from his hand.

"Poor bastard," Hunter says, shaking his head, which makes his hair brush against my ear. "He's gotta be taking this hard."

CHAPTER 4: HUNTER

"Skankology:
How Female Desperation Has Altered
the Julius Hook-Up Scene"

Aviva Roth for *The Julius Journal,* September

Let me tell you about Julius P. Heil High School. This place is pretty much a joke. Even the guy it's named after was a joke. Julius P. Heil was the governor of Wisconsin back in the day. I did a report on him freshman year, and according to my report, which I mostly got from Wikipedia, Julius was "known for clowning and silly antics." The guy our school is named after was known for being a clown. He did do some good stuff, though. Apparently, he really liked dairy products and promoted Wisconsin's cheese, which is really good cheese. Our school cheese is pretty awesome, too. Our cafeteria makes these amazing bacon-egg-and-cheese sandwiches that I eat almost every morning.

Other than our bacon-egg-and-cheeses, though, this place is a joke. There are about two hundred fifty kids total, so our principal likes to go around bragging about how much "individual attention" we all get, like it's a good thing. Individual attention is a *terrible* thing. If you skip one class, everyone knows about it. The teacher will track you down, or one of the guidance counselors will track you down and ask if you're smoking pot. According to the geniuses running this place, the only reason you would skip class is if you're smoking pot, though I actually find my classes more enjoyable when I'm high.

At Julius, it's easy to track down someone who's skipping class, because the building is a square made up of four hallways. You get trapped in it like a lab rat in a maze. So instead of skipping classes, I try to sleep through them instead. People think it's risky to sleep in class, but to be honest with ya, I manage to do it a lot.

Of course, the best you can hope for in class is a few five- to seven-minute catnaps. If you want some hardcore REM-cycle sleep, you gotta find some place out of the way. I used to sleep in the library, but then they installed cameras in the back of the library after an "incident." Apparently, someone got jerked off on the F volume of the *Encyclopædia Britannica*. Which is the most appropriate letter, I guess.

I tried out a bunch of different napping spots — cafeteria, gym locker room — but this year, I found the nirvana of the in-school napper: the band practice rooms. The rooms are pretty small, but they're good for sleeping. I actually am bummed out about the band. I really liked to play the drums.

I always got really into it. I mean, how many classes are there when you can sit in the back of the room banging on stuff? For me, just two: band and Mr. Castellano's computer class.

But I guess everything has a silver lining. There's no band, but there is a place for me to sleep.

"Huntro!"

Or not. Today I wake up to Eugene banging his hand against the glass door and staring at me. I've been sleeping stretched out in a chair with my feet up on the music stand.

"Let me in!" Eugene says.

"What time is it?" I ask Eugene as I open the door for him.

"The last bell just rang," Eugene tells me.

As soon as I let him in, I sit down and put my feet back up on the music stand. "Crap," I say. "I was supposed to go back to study hall."

"Here, look at this."

Eugene drops an envelope onto my stomach. When I open it, all this sparkly shit falls out of it and gets all over my shirt.

"What the hell is this?" I ask, standing up and brushing off my shirt.

"It's an invitation!" Eugene says, moving a music stand out of his way.

"No—what is this crap on it?"

"Glitter," Eugene says impatiently. "But read it! Read it!"

While I look at the invitation, Eugene bounces up and down on the balls of his feet.

"Back-to-school barbecue?" I say.

"It's the student senate's first social event of the year. A back-to-school barbecue for juniors and seniors. And you and I are going," Eugene tells me.

"What? We don't go to shit like this. We don't go to... glitter... activities."

I hand the invitation back to Eugene as he leads the way out of the practice room and into the main band room. I follow him out and sit on the lowest level of the bandstand.

"We are going," Eugene lectures me, waving the invitation in my face. Some glitter gets in my eye. Damn.

"This invitation was hand-delivered to me by *Bobbi Novak*."

Ahh, Bobbi Novak. It's kind of hard to describe how hot Bobbi Novak is. She's got these tits they should invent some kind of Nobel Prize for.

"She told me, 'I really, really hope you'll be there,'" Eugene says, with this dumb smirk on his face.

"She's on student senate. She organizes this kind of stuff," I tell him. "She wants everyone to show up."

Eugene leans against the grand piano and crosses his arms over his chest.

"I think she kinda likes me."

I shake my head. "There's no way in hell."

"*Last year*, there was no way in hell," Eugene says, pointing his finger at me. When he makes speeches, Eugene gets really expressive, pacing the floor and waving his hands around like a politician.

"*Last year*," Eugene repeats. "There was no way in hell. But this year, Bobbi's single. Justin Messina was her last boyfriend, and he's away at school. And a bunch of other guys are gone. All the McKennas are gone. All the Devines are gone. Huntro, we are in a boy recession."

Because I'm still picking glitter out of my arm hair, I'm only half paying attention.

"Huh? What?"

"We are in a boy recession," Eugene repeats. "There's been a sudden, drastic decrease in the male population at this school. And I'm gonna take advantage of it."

"Does a boy recession make you less ugly?"

From where I'm sitting, I grin up at Eugene. I call Eugene ugly to his face all the time. It sounds pretty harsh, but whatever, we're dudes. Plus, he has a crapload of money, so he can deal with me calling him ugly.

"No," Eugene says, pretty much ignoring my comment. "But a recession changes people. They don't have the same options they did before. They have to reexamine their priorities."

"You mean lower their standards?"

Eugene stops pacing to glare at me.

"No," he says. "Because of this boy recession, Bobbi has the chance to see me in a different way. Sure, I'm not an athlete. I'm not on the student senate. I'm not —"

"Tall, good-looking, funny, sexually experienced..."

From the second level of the bandstand, where he's been pacing, Eugene kicks me in the back. "Stop!" I tell him, falling over onto my side, half laughing. "Stop! I think those are my kidneys!"

"Seriously, Huntro," Eugene says, sitting down next to me. "I've been investing in the stock market since I was eleven, and I know a good opportunity when I see one. This is my chance. I'm going to that barbecue, and I'm gonna show Bobbi that I'm a good guy. I would do anything for this girl, Huntro. Anything."

I look over at him. He's completely serious, despite the glitter on his face.

"All right, Mr. Pluskota," I say, kicking off my leather flip-flops. "I'll go with you. When is it?"

"Tomorrow night." Eugene claps me on the shoulder. "Your confidence means a lot, man."

I don't tell him the reason I'm gonna go to this barbecue is to watch him crash and burn. But who knows? It doesn't have to be a disaster. Bobbi Novak's a pretty nice girl. I think she'll let him down gently.

"So what's the plan?" I ask. "What's the game plan, stud?"

"I've been asking around to find out what girls are into," Eugene tells me, really pleased with himself. "So I'm gonna get a spray tan and make red-velvet cupcakes."

Well, this barbecue should be interesting. I'll get to see if Eugene's boy-recession theory pans out. And if it doesn't, at least I'll get a cupcake out of it.

CHAPTER 5: KELLY

*"Boy Recession 101:
How Julius Girls Can Make the Best
of a Bad Ratio"*

Aviva Roth for *The Julius Journal*, September

I'm gonna punch Diva Price in the face," Aviva announces, coming back from the s'mores table with three marshmallows on a big pointy stick, which she's waving around in a way that makes her threat actually threatening.

The back-to-school barbecue is the only Julius event other than graduation during which it's warm enough to wear short shorts — which is why it's Aviva's favorite. It's one of my favorites, too. I love that good bonfire smell, the picnic setup, and the s'mores, especially the ones with marshmallows that are burned on the outside and super-gooey on the inside. I've eaten two of them already tonight, and I want another one.

"Hey, watch that thing." Darcy grabs the end of Aviva's

stick. "No one is losing an eye tonight. *Or* getting punched in the face."

I guess Darcy wants to keep marshmallow-related violence to a minimum, seeing as it's her first back-to-school barbecue as school president. But she kept a pretty close eye on things last year as vice president, because Charlie Devine was too busy popping the collar of his polo shirt to be very effective.

"What did Diva do?" I ask Aviva, pulling the top marshmallow off her stick and popping it into my mouth.

"She Tweeted that I lied about being biracial now that it's cool because of Obama."

"It's not *cool* because of Obama," Darcy says. "The fact that we have a biracial president has political ramifications beyond—"

"Just ignore her," I tell Aviva, cutting Darcy off. "Diva is so ridiculous with her Tweeting and her creepy close-up Facebook pictures. The only reason anyone friends her is to mercilessly mock her."

Diva Price is one of the notorious Julius spandexers. Her name is actually Dina, but after she starred in a lice-shampoo commercial when she was nine, she started making everyone call her Diva because she considers herself an actress/model. None of us consider her an actress or a model, seeing as that lice-shampoo commercial was her only gig ever, but we do consider her to be a diva, so that's what we call her. Diva is the chief inquisitor of the panty-line persecutions, and she squeezes herself into the tightest synthetic pants possible and wears them stubbornly through the Wisconsin winter, when everyone else throws in the towel and turns to long johns and unflattering thermal layers. Right now, Diva is over by the s'mores table, posing for a picture with this cute senior, Peter Chung, both of them holding sticks with marshmallows on them.

"No, that's not the right angle," Diva says to Amy Schiffer, the redheaded senior spandexer who's taking the picture. "Give it to me."

Diva grabs Amy's digital camera out of her hand and changes the setting. After that, Amy tries again. When the flash goes off, Diva grabs the camera.

"Ew! That is *so* gross," Diva says. "Amy, you suck at taking pictures. We need someone tall—where's Josh?"

Josh Long is another cute, tall senior. In fact, Josh and Chung are two of the only cute tall Julius boys left. There are always more girls than boys at stuff like this, but this year is extreme, and Josh and Chung look like the only two redwoods left standing after a forest fire.

Aviva stands up to watch Diva pose.

"Be careful, Josh!" Aviva calls out across the fire, as Josh takes the camera. "Those things tend to break around Diva!"

Through the bonfire smoke, Diva glares at Aviva and sticks out her tongue, at which point Josh snaps the picture.

"*Joshhhh!*" Diva whines.

That cheers Aviva up.

"Hey, is anyone covering this for the paper?" I ask her.

"Oh, good news!" Aviva says. "They stopped printing the school newspaper!"

"What?" Darcy asks. "No one told me about that!"

"Ms. Graham just told us today," Aviva says. "She gave us this whole speech about going green and saving paper. But chances are, the cheap-ass gene kicked in."

"That's ridiculous!" I say. "They can't do this to you, Viva. Journalism is the only class in which you can make use of the hours you spend reading *Cosmo* and *Teen Vogue* instead of doing your homework."

"Well, I was pissed at first," Aviva says, taking her last bite of marshmallow. "But remember that rant I posted on my blog about all the guys leaving our school? I got tons of hits and thought, why don't we just put the newspaper online? So we are! Ms. Graham liked my idea so much that she gave me my own column! And then she kinda looked like she regretted it...."

Aviva writes about the social scene for *The Julius Journal.* Last year she submitted a Valentine's Day article titled "Fourteen Fun Things to Do with Whipped Cream" to Ms. Graham, the journalism teacher. Let's just say there was not one mention of cake in it.

"What's your column gonna be about?" Darcy asks.

"I don't know," Aviva says. "I need a catchy title, or a concept, like... *Ow!*"

Aviva whips her head around.

"Did you just throw a stick at me?" she demands. Diva, who's trying to sit on a blanket in a tiny denim skirt without flashing everyone — or maybe not trying that hard — just shrugs.

"Oops," she says, and gives Aviva a fake smile.

Aviva turns back to us, growling. "Maybe I should write a column about arch nemesises."

"Arch neme*ses*," Darcy corrects her. "But yeah, if you do, you can include mine."

Darcy nods toward Diva's blanket, where Bobbi Novak is bending over to kiss each of her fellow spandexers on the cheek. Bobbi Novak is the social chair of the student senate — and the reason so many people show up to events like this. Bobbi looks like a cross between a Barbie doll and a Kardashian — she's blond and tiny but with big boobs and a bubble butt. Bobbi's boobs and butt are real, but everything else about her is fake — her hair extensions, her tan, and the glitter all over her skin. Actually, I'm not sure about the glitter. Judging by Bobbi's personality, she could have been born, literally, sparkly. It wouldn't surprise me.

"Hi, girlies!" She waves as she passes our blanket. "Hope you're having fun! Have some s'mores — they're yummy!"

Darcy considers Bobbi to be the second most annoying ditz in the world, after Elle Woods in *Legally Blonde*, but Aviva and I don't mind her too much. She's one of the better spandexers, in my opinion. Diva, Amy, and Amy's best frenemy Pam Bausch-Farber can all be super-fake and manipulative, and Bobbi isn't like that. At least she's friendly.

"What about you, Kell?" Aviva asks, standing up and brushing off her shorts. "Any arch neme*sees* you want me to write about?"

I don't have any, because I get along with everyone, even the meanest spandexers. Last year in Spanish class, Pam asked me to cover for her when she went into Milwaukee to meet up with a college guy. I asked her why she didn't use Amy as her cover, seeing as she and Amy were actually friends (except when they were fighting), and Pam said, "My mom likes you. My mom is always like, 'Kelly Robbins is such a *nice* girl.'"

When Pam said *nice*, she rolled her eyes and pronounced it like it was an annoying skin disease she didn't want to catch from me. Being nice is boring.

"The second wave of people is arriving!" Darcy says, popping up from the blanket. "Do you think there's enough soda? I'm gonna go check the tables."

Making our way back to the snack table, we check out the second-wavers, who probably showed up late to prove they're too cool for school events. Most of them are standing on the edge of the woods trying to smoke without getting caught by the school chaperones, and a few of the boys we call the gas-station gang, because they spend Friday nights hanging out on the corner by the gas station, look like they might be drunk. Hunter is with them, but he doesn't look drunk and he's eating a s'more.

"Look over at the drinks table!" Aviva gasps. "Oh my God! Look at them!"

"What?" I ask, turning back to the tables. And then I see them.

Behind the drinks table, Bobbi Novak takes a really big bite of a really big cupcake and squeals, "These are, like, super-delish! Like, *super*-delish!"

"I baked them myself," Eugene Pluskota tells her proudly, peeling the tinfoil back from the tray to reveal three rows of perfectly frosted cupcakes.

I'm surprised that Eugene is even at the back-to-school barbecue, and I'm even more surprised that he's brought baked goods. I don't think I've ever seen Eugene with a girl before. Actually, that's not true. Eugene has hit on girls, but it was always in such a creepy, perverted way that the girls ran away immediately. Like during the freshman laser-tag trip, when Eugene kept groping Aviva in the dark and asking, "Is this base? Is this base?"

But it doesn't look like Bobbi is getting creeped out, because she's licking frosting off her pinky finger and admitting with a giggle, "I don't even know what red velvet *is*. It's my favorite flavor, and I don't even know what it *is*! I know there's not real *velvet* in there, but..."

"Dutch cocoa," Eugene informs her. "And the red is food coloring. They're not naturally red."

"No way!" Bobbi says, batting her fake eyelashes in surprise.

I can't believe what I'm hearing.

"Are Bobbi and Eugene *flirting?*" I ask Darcy and Aviva.

"No way," Darcy says immediately, neatly capping her s'more with a perfectly square graham cracker. "Eugene is being a pervert, and Bobbi is being nicer than she should be."

"I don't know," I say. "It actually looks like Bobbi is flirting with *him.*"

As I say that, Bobbi lifts her cupcake up to Eugene's mouth, and he takes a bite. Then Bobbi brings it to her mouth and takes a bite, right from the *same side of the cupcake.* I turn and hiss at Darcy, "She just took a bite out of his bite!"

Darcy looks disgusted and alarmed, like Eugene's carrying the swine flu and this is the start of a worldwide epidemic.

Having read at least fifty magazine articles on decoding body language, Aviva considers herself to be an expert, and she's been analyzing Bobbi and Eugene carefully.

"Look at her twirling her hair," Aviva says. "That could be flirting. But if she touches him, she's *definitely* flirting."

It's getting crowded on this side of the fire, so we can't hear what either of them is saying, but Eugene is talking a lot, and Bobbi is twirling her ponytail so hard I'm scared her extensions will fall out. Then Eugene says something and Bobbi starts to giggle...and she puts her hand on his arm. *Yup. Definitely flirting.*

Aviva fishes her yellow reporter's notepad out of her giant purse and turns to me.

"Kelly, go find out what's happening between Bobbi and Eugene. Just ask Hunter," Aviva insists.

"What?" I say.

"He's always with Eugene. He must know what's going on."

"Why do I have to ask him?"

"You guys are friends," Darcy says. "Aren't you in band together?"

"Band doesn't even exist anymore."

"But you've seen"—Aviva wiggles her fingers in front of my face like she's casting a spell on me—"*the face beneath the hair.*"

I give in, but I refuse to bring the reporter's notebook over. Hunter is near the bonfire with his friends Derek Palewski and Dave Cheney, who we call Pirate Dave because he always wears a red-and-white striped shirt. As I walk over now, Derek takes advantage of the fact that the chaperones are busting someone for smoking in the woods, and throws a soda can into the fire. When it shoots up a bunch of sparks, Derek yells hoarsely in triumph and Hunter laughs.

"Hey, Hunter."

Hunter turns around. "Hey, Kelly. What's up?"

"Not much. What are you guys doing?"

"Just enjoying Derek's, uh, pyromaniac antics."

Hunter's been standing close to the fire and he's kinda sweaty. As he pushes his damp hair off his forehead, I notice that he's actually kind of cute underneath all that hair, and his blue eyes are really bright in the light from the bonfire.

"Darcy and Viva wanna know what Eugene's doing with Bobbi," I say. "They sent me over here to be nosy."

"Oh, man, yeah! Are they still talking?"

Hunter leans back to get a better view of the drinks table, where Bobbi is collecting empty soda cans and Eugene is holding the recycling bin for her. Seeing that, Hunter shakes his head and lets out a long whistle.

"I can't believe she's falling for his bullshit."

"What do you mean?"

Hunter pushes his hair back again. "Eugene's got this whole plan to get Bobbi."

"A plan? Did he put something in the cupcakes?" I ask, lowering my voice.

Hunter lowers his voice, too, and sounds completely amazed when he says, "He put *Dutch cocoa* in them. He seriously baked them all by himself!"

He's so serious that I burst out laughing. I was talking about roofies, and Hunter is impressed by Eugene's baking skills.

"So that's Eugene's plan?" I ask. "The way to a girl's heart is through her stomach?"

"I dunno if he's going for her heart," Hunter says. "But

he thinks she'll be willing to go out with him because of the boy recession."

"Wait, because of the *recession*?"

"The boy recession," Hunter corrects me, kicking a stick toward the fire. His sneakers have no laces in them.

"What is the boy recession?"

"You know how all those dudes left our school? Like, the football guys? Eugene calls it the boy recession."

"And he thinks he has a chance with Bobbi because..."

"He thinks girls are gonna, like, take what they can get, now that there aren't that many dudes hanging around."

Well, that part is definitely true — there aren't too many dudes hanging around. I see only Derek, who's begging people for coins to throw into the bonfire; Pirate Dave, who's threatening Derek with a stick; and Damian Weiss, a nice nerdy boy. But for every boy, there are at least three girls. And over on their beach towels, Josh and Chung are completely surrounded by girls. "I thought Eugene was an idiot," Hunter admits, stretching his arms over his head so far that his T-shirt pulls up, revealing his flat, almost hairless stomach. "I never think anything really changes like that. But now, I mean, I dunno. Look at them!"

Bobbi and Eugene are toasting marshmallows, and their shoulders are touching as they hold their sticks close to the fire. Everyone is watching them now. Behind me, a spandexer stops texting to stare at Bobbi and Eugene.

"Oh my God," she says, in a hushed whisper. "She *gave him her marshmallow*."

Her friend turns to her and asks, "Is it me, or does Eugene look a little cuter this year?"

I tell Hunter I'll see him later. I've gotta get back to Darcy and Aviva and let them know that the situation is bigger than just Eugene and Bobbi. *The Boy Recession.* I think I've got a name for Aviva's column, too.

CHAPTER 6: HUNTER

"Quarterback, Not Sexy Back:
Julius Football Team Lacks Athletic Skills, Hotness"

"The Boy Recession©" by Aviva Roth,
The Julius Journal, September

*W*ow. *There are a lot of active people out here.*

I'm on my longboard, heading out to the football field behind Julius, and I see all these people running, sweating, and hitting one another with sticks. The cross-country runners are coming at me in this huge pack, huffing and puffing like crazy, and on the tennis court, Bobbi Novak is practicing her killer serve.

I'm not usually out on the sports fields after school, but a few minutes ago, Derek texted me *You gotta see this,* and told me to come out to the football field. I'm betting fifty bucks he's trying to skateboard off the bleachers again. Last time he broke his arm in two places.

Derek is on the bleachers, but he's not jumping off them. He's just lounging, hanging out with Dave and Damian. The three of them are in this nonexistent band called the D-Bags. Freshman year, the three of them decided it would be cool to start a band, but they never actually bothered to learn to play any instruments.

"What's up?" I say, climbing onto the bleachers.

"We're watching football tryouts," Derek tells me, squinting up at me from under the brim of his hat.

"This sucks," Dave adds. "They need to put pads on. No one is hitting each other."

Dave's always muttering under his breath, but we're used to it and just ignore him.

"Tryouts?" I say. "What the hell? Doesn't the season start, like, next week?"

"Four of our starters transferred," Damian tells me.

Damian's a good guy, and he knows a surprising shit-load about football, even though he spends most of his time in his basement, playing *World of Warcraft*.

"So they've gotta move up the guys from the bench," Damian says.

"And they've gotta recruit new schmucks to sit on the bench," Dave says.

"One of which is…" Derek says as he points his arm toward the field.

I turn around and shield my eyes from the sun. The guys on the field are getting into position, wearing those dumb nylon jerseys we have to wear in gym class, and our dumb gym teacher, who always blows his whistle too loud and is our new football coach, is out there. That's when I see him.

"What?" I balk, turning back to Derek. "What the hell? Eugene is out there?"

Derek's leaning back against the bleachers with both of his arms outstretched, and he's got the biggest grin on his face.

"Eugene's out there."

"He's trying out for the football team? Is this a joke? Is he trying to bust everyone's balls?"

"He's trying out for the football team," Derek says, nodding.

"They really need guys," Damian says. "They're desperate. The coach even tried to recruit Dave."

"As if," mutters Dave. "Fuckers."

"Obviously, Dave told them to fuck off." Derek laughs. "But Eugene embraced it as part of his master plan."

"He thinks he's gonna get into Bobbi's pants," Dave says. "But he's not."

"So, what, Eugene thinks that girls only give it up to big, manly football players?" I say.

"No, you antifeminist," Derek corrects me. "Bobbi's on the tennis team, and the tennis team and football team work out at the same time. They'll be hitting the gym together."

Down on the field, Eugene's sprinting up and down the sidelines. After about three sprints, he looks winded. I sit down next to Derek, who's taken his lighter out of his pocket and is flipping it up over and over with his thumb.

"Hey," I say to him. "How do you know all this? When did Eugene tell you about his master plan?"

Derek shrugs. "Last week. He took me out, and we had a heart-to-heart. He bought me waffle fries."

"Dammit," I say, shaking my hair into my eyes to block out the sun. "Eugene's supposed to have heart-to-hearts with me. He's supposed to buy *me* food."

Shrugging, Derek says, "He said he called you, but you were asleep."

Down on the field, the recruits are in position, and Eugene got put on the defensive line. Guys on the defensive line face the biggest guys on the field — the offensive linemen. Eugene, who's neither built like a brick wall nor particularly fast, isn't the best fit for the position. Right as the whistle blows, he charges forward and heads directly for Chung, who's playing offense.

And that, ladies and gentlemen, is how you get a black eye in touch football.

Meanwhile, all of us on the bleachers start to laugh. "Maybe we should be taping this for YouTube," Derek says.

"Maybe we should be calling my chiropractor," Damian says, sounding genuinely worried.

Once the excitement is over, the other guys take off, but I wait around for Eugene, who makes it through the rest of the tryout and even hangs out afterward, trying to be "the man," slapping hands with all the guys on the team.

"Yo, Tim Tebow!" I call to him from the fence. "Let's move it along here."

Finally he gets off the field, and we head back to the school together. I'm on my longboard, weaving along the path, and Eugene's walking next to me, chugging Gatorade.

"How'd I look out there?" Eugene asks me, in between huge gulps.

"Well..." I tilt my heels back so the longboard turns away from Eugene. Just then, Bobbi comes off the tennis court at the same time we're walking by.

"Hi, Eugene! Hi, Hunter!" she says, coming toward us, holding her racket. "Hunter, are you trying out, too?"

"For the football team? *Nooooo*," I tell her, shaking my hair into my face.

"You should!" Bobbi encourages. "They need guys! And you look like you're in good shape!"

I just kinda laugh. I'm in terrible shape.

Speaking of people who are in terrible shape, Eugene asks Bobbi, "How was practice? Did you get the new serve down?"

"Not totally perfect," Bobbi says, shaking her head. Her forehead is all sweaty, but even her sweat is sexy. "But how was practice for you? How was the first day of tryouts?"

"I think everyone was impressed," Eugene says, all serious and thoughtful. "Those calf exercises we did together, I really felt those. I was pretty quick off the blocks, ya know?"

"Foot speed is important," Bobbi agrees, nodding. "We'll do more of those tomorrow."

Eugene turns to me and explains, "I told Bobbi I was trying out for the team, so she took me to the gym this weekend to show me how to work out. She's been giving me some great tips on building muscle."

"Uh-huh," I say, grinning.

"And *you* were supposed to bring me that mineral bath soak," Bobbi says. "My sore muscles need it!" When she says *you*, she pokes Eugene in the shoulder and laughs.

"I will!" Eugene says. "Text me to remind me!"

I'm seriously impressed. I mean, Eugene put his seduction plan into action on Friday night; it's only Monday, and he's already got Bobbi's number, *and* her workout tips. As Bobbi walks Eugene and me back toward the school, I realize the weirdest part of this conversation isn't the fact that Eugene takes baths. Instead, it's that I think it's possible that Bobbi Novak might be—as Derek would say— feelin' the kid.

CHAPTER 7: HUNTER

"Male Point of View Underrepresented at Julius Due to Student Senate's Overwhelming Female Majority"

"The Boy Recession©" by Aviva Roth,
The Julius Journal, October

I always liked meetings with my guidance counselor. They get you out of class. Plus, the guidance office is awesome. It has these cinnamon plug-in air fresheners, so it always smells like Christmas. Plus, my guidance counselor, Ms. Duff, keeps a bowl of candy on her desk. She's got some good stuff in there, like little bags of Sour Patch Kids.

My meetings with Ms. Duff have pretty much followed the same pattern since freshman year. She asks me, "How are you *doing?*" in this understanding voice and tries to figure out if I've got any big emotional crisis going on. I never do, which I think disappoints her.

Then she'll talk about how awesome my standardized test scores are. I do pretty well on those kinds of tests—the ones you don't have to study for. I kicked ass on the PSATs. At my meeting in the spring, Ms. Duff said I was "highly gifted" and called me a "natural test taker." She showed me all these charts that said I was some kind of math genius. She moved me up to precalculus and signed me up for AP chem.

Usually, after she strokes my ego, she gives me a pep talk about putting more effort into my homework and essays and all that crap.

This meeting seems different, though. It's October now, which is when juniors are supposed to start planning for college applications. Maybe it's because meetings about college stuff are supposed to be intense, or maybe Ms. Duff is stressed out because the other guidance counselor left, but I'm getting a bad vibe from her. First of all, the candy bowl is missing. Even worse, Ms. Duff is armed with her Fahrenbach file, which has all my grades and test scores in it, and she launches right into the investigation.

"What happened on this precalculus test last week, Mr. Fahrenbach?" Ms. Duff asks. "Can you tell me why you got a sixty-eight?"

"Uh…well…that was a pretty tough test," I say. "There were some trick questions at the end, I think. Everyone in the class was, like, freaking out."

"The class average was a ninety-two."

She also has the class averages for every test, quiz, and essay from this year. *Faaaantastic.*

"When are you going to complete this lab report for

AP chemistry? Why were you late for U.S. history every day last week? Why didn't you participate in the President's Physical Fitness Test?"

Man, I've got to get some excuses going. I can't tell Ms. Duff that I skipped the President's Physical Fitness Test to sit in the locker room and eat a White Castle burger.

"Well, for me, it's like..."

I try to pull myself up so I'm sitting straight in the chair, so I look more serious. But the chair is really soft leather, so I'm still slouching.

"What about this pop quiz in humanities?" Ms. Duff demands.

"Yeah, I..."

Ms. Duff looks up from the file. "Honestly, Hunter," she begins—I'm Hunter now, instead of Mr. Fahrenbach—"you shouldn't even be taking this humanities course. You should be in AP English."

Ms. Duff shuts the Fahrenbach file.

"Hunter," she says, "I am now the guidance counselor for every single student at this school. I know everyone's abilities. I know everyone's grades. So I know that you are more intelligent than ninety-five percent of the students here.

"But almost every single one of them," Ms. Duff continues, "is trying harder than you."

I don't want to look Ms. Duff in the eyes, but everything I look at in this office reminds me what a slacker I am—the college pennants, the books about writing a killer résumé.

"What about extracurriculars?" Ms. Duff asks.

"Um, I'm in the band," I say. "But...I guess that's... The band doesn't exist anymore. But I still play! I play the guitar, too, at home. And I write some stuff. I write some of my own music."

"Okay, that's good," Ms. Duff says, nodding. But she doesn't write anything down. "Is there anything you can do with music? Any way to show your leadership skills?"

"Leadership skills?" I ask. "Like, uh, conducting an orchestra or something?"

"Maybe organizing a concert for senior citizens at a nursing home? Fund-raising to buy instruments for under-privileged kids?" Ms. Duff says. "You need to connect to other people. You need to show colleges that you're involved with your community. You must care about something, Hunter."

"Well, I care about music. I do."

"It's time to prove it," Ms. Duff says. Then she stands up behind her desk and extends her hand. I don't think a teacher has ever tried to shake my hand before, but I try to hide my surprise and give her a firm handshake, because Eugene's always lecturing me about how important it is to give a firm handshake.

As I push open the double doors to the hallway and breathe in the normal, bad-smelling hallway air, I see

Kelly and Chung's sister Kristin coming out of the nurse's office.

"Here you go," Kelly says, handing Kristin a coat and two books. "This is what was in your locker. Is there anything else?"

Kristin is coughing up a lung, and Kelly reaches out and touches her back and says, "Feel better, okay? Lemme know if you need anything."

Suddenly a lightbulb goes on in my head. This is exactly who I need right now. Kelly and I have been in band together since freshman year, and we have a bunch of other classes together, too. She's always showing up to class on time and lending people pencils. I sprint down the hallway toward Kelly and stop short right in front of her.

"Hunter!" she says, surprised to look up and have me panting right in her face. "Are you okay? I don't think I've ever seen you...run...before."

"I'm good," I say. "I'm really good. I was just thinking...I've been thinking about the music program. Ya know, the kids not learning music. Remember? In the band room?"

"Yeah, of course, the third-graders," Kelly says.

"I want to do it," I tell her. "Let's do the thing, the peer thing. Let's teach them. You and me."

"We should!" Kelly says. "We should start figuring it out. Maybe for next year? We'd have to get permission, and find a teacher who would—"

"No! Let's do it this year. Let's get some instruments, get some kids, and get going."

Kelly smiles, and her eyes crinkle up at the edges. That sounds weird, or not cute, but it's actually really cute.

"Okay, I don't know how long it will take to get going," she says, laughing a little bit. "But we can get going."

CHAPTER 8: KELLY

"Opposites Attract:
What Makes Unlikely Couples Tick"

"The Boy Recession©" by Aviva Roth,
The Julius Journal, October

"**W**hich one of you is flam tap?" Hunter asks. "And which one is paradiddle?"

It's third period on a Thursday in mid-October, and Hunter is holding a drumstick in each hand and pacing the bandstand behind three of our third-graders, who are sitting in chairs with drum pads on their laps. One is this tiny girl with two pigtails that stick straight out of her head, and the other two are boys—one calm and one with no front teeth.

"I'm flam tap!" No-Teeth Kid says, raising his hand and drumstick really high in the air.

Hunter takes his sticks and poises them over No-Teeth Kid's head. Gently, he taps the kid's head with each stick in rapid succession, saying, "flam," and then with only the right stick, saying, "tap."

No-Teeth Kid loves getting hit in the head — even really, really lightly. When Hunter is done, the third-grader tilts his head back and gives Hunter a gummy smile.

"Now you guys try it," Hunter says. "All of you. *Flam tap.*"

Hunter's three students tighten their grips on their drumsticks and repeat on their drum pads what Hunter did on their heads. When they pronounce "flam tap," they sound awed, as if "flam tap" were a spell from a Harry Potter movie. Actually, it's a rudiment — one of the basic patterns you start with when you're learning the drums.

"Awesome! You guys got it!" Hunter says. "Now it's time for the paradiddle. Your head ready, Molly?"

This is how Hunter teaches music. Today isn't even the first time he's hit the kids on the head. Last week, during the first lesson, he taught his students to hold drumsticks and then set them free to run around the room, hitting things. Anything they want — the blackboard, the floor, the music stands, one another...

"Hear how something hollow has a different pitch?" Hunter yelled to them over the racket. "The blackboard has that tinny sound when you hit it, but the wall sounds different. Here, c'mere, hit the wall."

For his second lesson, Hunter walked his kids to the top level of the bandstand and showed them all the parts of the drum kit. Then he assigned one student to the cymbals, one to the bass drum, and one to the snare drum.

"This is a contest," he announced. "Which one of you can be *loudest*?"

And then, on Tuesday, he found out that if you hit an eight-year-old on the head on purpose, they think it's really, really funny.

The fact that we don't have a faculty adviser in the room while we're teaching music is good for Hunter. His lesson plans would probably fall apart if you took away that element of danger. But it means that I have to be the responsible one, because I worry that if someone gets a concussion and their parents sue our school, this music program will definitely be canceled.

"Um, Hunter?" I call across the room. "Can you guys maybe get to the drum-pad part of the lesson?"

"Oh, yeah." Hunter grins and tosses his hair back. He jumps down from the bandstand and jogs to the piano to grab his own drum pad, calling out while his back is turned, "Loosen up that grip, flam tap!"

So this is PMS. No, we don't have a better name for it yet — and yes, I know we need one. For the past two weeks, Hunter and I have had fun talking about PMS in the hallways and having people give us strange looks, but I don't plan on listing PMS on my college applications next year. The only person who could legitimately do that is Pam, who spends so much time with actual PMS that it's an extracurricular activity for her.

Every Tuesday and Thursday, nine third-graders come over from the elementary school on a bus. Hunter and I walk them to the band room and give them lessons in drums or the flute. The room is back the way I like it—

there's music, laughter, and lots of noise; the instruments our kids rented are in the cubbies.

That day in the hallway, when Hunter told me we should start the music program ourselves, he surprised me. I had no idea he was that interested. When he and I asked our friends from band to help teach, all of them had either signed up for another class or liked having a study hall so much they wouldn't give it up, which made me realize that Hunter had given up his study hall. Before our first lesson, he told me he'd never worked with kids before, or babysat, or anything, but our students loved him right away. He's super-patient and so easygoing that he can even deal with No-Teeth Kid, whom I personally think could use some Ritalin.

Setting the program up wasn't exactly the easiest process in the world, though. When we first met to go over the details, I brought a two-page to-do list, and he brought a bag of Cheetos.

"I think we should figure out instrument rentals first," I said. "So we can put that information in when we mail out the permission slips to the parents."

"Right, the instruments," Hunter said. "Well, there's a drum set in the band room already, so I'm good."

"But they don't start on the drum set when they're first learning, do they? I thought you used those drum-pad things."

"Oh, right, the drum pads," Hunter said, his mouth full of Cheetos. "I still have mine; they can use it."

"But we might need a lot of them," I said.

"How many?"

"We don't know how many kids are signed up," I said. "We won't know until we get the permission slips back."

"True, right, you're right," Hunter said. "So let's find some instruments to rent. Should we just, like, Google places?"

At that point, I realized I was going to have to handle most of that to-do list: the permission slips, the coordination of the bus from the elementary school, the program proposal to the school board.

Sometimes I get so distracted thinking about all the things I haven't done that I forget about actually teaching. Like right now.

"Kelly," one of my students says and looks up at me. "Can I stop blowing now? I have a headache."

One of my redheaded twins has been trying over and over to make a sound with her flute, and she's light-headed. *Poor girl.*

"Yes! Yes, take a break," I tell her, patting her head. "We're gonna work on reading music. Everyone take out a crayon! Who remembers what a C looks like?"

Not only have I been doing all the PMS paperwork, I actually have twice as many kids to teach as Hunter does. That's not his fault, though. And I volunteered to put my name on all the permission slips, and the contract with the bus driver, and the proposal we submitted to Dr. Nicholas. But that was after Hunter told me he wasn't sure Dr.

Nicholas would trust him with a room full of eight-year-olds armed with sticks.

"I don't think he likes me that much," Hunter told me hesitantly, the day before we were supposed to talk to Dr. Nicholas. "Last time I was in that office, he threatened to suspend me."

"What? Why?"

"Well, freshman year I got one of those UNICEF boxes, you know? How you go trick-or-treating for UNICEF and collect money from everyone? I did that, but I didn't hand in the box. I just totally forgot, because it was under all this crap in my locker, so...then, remember how they brought those, like, drug dogs to school to go through the lockers?"

I guess I had a totally horrified look on my face, because Hunter started crossing his arms in front of himself, like he was canceling what he just said.

"No, no, no," he said. "Not anything like that, no. They just opened all the lockers, and they found my UNICEF box in there, like, five months later. That was it. It's not as bad as you think."

"Yeah, you were just embezzling money from kids in the third world."

"No!" Hunter protested, but when our eyes met, we both started laughing. And in the end, whether Dr. Nicholas likes him or not, Hunter has turned out to be a great teacher.

"So that's one flam tap, two paradiddles, and a flam

tap at the end," Hunter says. "Are we ready for it? One, two, one-two-three-four..."

Knocking his drumsticks together over his head, Hunter counts off.

"You did it! Awesome! Rock and roll!" Hunter says, giving them high fives.

"Okay, everyone, time to pack up!" I say, standing. "Put your instruments in your cubbies. The bus is already outside."

After we load the kids into the bus, I return to the band room and notice that the freshman boy with the nice sweaters is holding the door open.

"Hi!" I say to him. "You're the piccolo!"

"Um..." He smiles. "Yeah. I'm Johann."

Johann is pretty attractive for a freshman. He definitely looks young, but he's cute — and probably foreign, with a name like Johann.

"I was hoping I could help out with the music program," he says, very formally, with his hands in the pockets of his neatly ironed khakis.

"Really? You want to?"

I'm so excited that my voice squeaks, which is embarrassingly amplified because of the band room's acoustics.

"I can teach, if you want," he says. "I've given flute lessons and piano lessons before, and some percussion. And my dad is a music professor, so I have a bunch of theory books."

"Music theory! We haven't even thought about that."

"Well, I don't have to..."

"No, we should! We should be doing that!"

"But if you already have teachers, I can just help out and do paperwork, or whatever you need," Johann says. "I guess I'm pretty responsible."

Responsible. That is exactly what I need. Johann will let me be my Libra self. He'll be super-responsible, Hunter will be slightly irresponsible, and I'll make sure everyone gets along.

"Oh my gosh, I love you!" I exclaim.

Johann, embarrassed, looks down at his clogs. I don't think he's the kind of guy you should declare your love for.

CHAPTER 9: HUNTER

*"Girls' Teams Dominate at Homecoming:
Femme Fatales of Fall Sports"*

"The Boy Recession©" by Aviva Roth,
The Julius Journal, October

What is all this crap?

It's late October, and I've fallen into my habit of arriving to first period fifteen minutes late. But this morning, my dad dropped me off only ten minutes late, so I figured I had time to go to the cafeteria for a bacon-egg-and-cheese.

But when I turn from the main hallway down south, there are green streamers all over and balloons strewn across the floor, impeding my way to bacon-egg-and-cheese. In the cafeteria, I notice another weird thing: Eugene and Chung wearing matching suits.

"Yo, Scarface!" I yell with my mouth full.

I pay for my half-eaten sandwich and walk over to Eugene and Chung.

"Happy homecoming, *mio fratello!*" Eugene greets me.

"What's going on with this?" I ask him, gesturing to the two of them and their suits.

"With what?" Eugene asks.

But he knows what, because he presses the lapels of his jacket smooth and reaches for his shirt cuffs to make sure they're sticking out of his jacket sleeves.

"You finally figure out how to clone yourself?" I say, looking from him to Chung.

Chung looks down at Eugene, confused.

"Dude, I'm, like, a foot taller than him," Chung tells me.

"And you're Asian," Eugene adds. He turns to me and asks, "You like my special game-day suit? This isn't one of my regular suits. We got these specially made for homecoming."

Eugene's on the football team now. He still sucks as much as ever, but they took all the guys who tried out, because they were so desperate to fill up the roster. The team has played three games so far, and lost every one. Eugene sits on the bench, but he feels like a badass because he gets to hang out with Chung and those guys.

"You guys go shopping together?" I ask them.

"I got us all a deal from Brooks Brothers," Eugene says. "They're our team's corporate sponsor now. The Senators, brought to you by Brooks Brothers."

"The Senators? What Senators?"

"Our school mascot, Huntro," Eugene says. "What are you, a Brazilian exchange student? How long have you been at this school?"

"I sleep through a lot of stuff," I tell him. Then I think about it for a second and laugh.

"The Senators. Really intimidating," I tell them. "Look at you guys. You look like fuckin' senators. I bet you kick some ass in those ties."

"Hey!" Chung points his finger at me. "These ties are Italian silk."

"Happy homecoming!"

Bobbi Novak comes bouncing up to us. She's got her team warm-ups on, and she's drinking some healthy protein thingy.

"Happy homecoming!" Eugene exclaims, and throws open his arms, forcing Bobbi to hug him. She goes right up and presses her miracle tits against his damned Italian silk tie.

"Were you so tired this morning?" Bobbi asks Eugene.

"We were all up 'til midnight last night, decorating the hallways," Eugene explains to me.

"Hunter, you have to give us your unbiased opinion," Bobbi says. "What do you think of the decorations?"

She looks really excited to hear what I think, so I say, "Uhhh...I like the balloons."

"Yay!" Bobbi claps her hand against her protein-drink thingy. "Then it was totally worth it! We were up so late, I just hope I have enough energy for my match this afternoon."

Eugene jumps in as soon as she says that.

"Your match is at four, right?" he says. "I can make it, I've just gotta sprint back to our team dinner as soon as it's over."

"And *I'm* going to, like, sprint home and shower in between my game and your game," Bobbi says, laughing. "You're coming tonight, right, Hunter? We can be, like, a cheering section for Eugene!"

Before I answer, I look back and forth from Bobbi to the smug bastard in the Italian silk tie.

"You gonna root for me, Huntro?" Eugene asks suggestively, wiggling his eyebrows.

I grin. "Oh, I'll be cheering you on," I tell him. "I really hope you score."

"Raise your right hand if you're a little gingerbread boy who got injured on the bench," I say to Eugene.

It's Friday night, and I'm standing on the football field sidelines, holding Eugene's helmet by the face mask with one hand and a bag of Cracker Jack in the other. In front of me, Eugene is lying on a white stretcher in his full football uniform — cleats, white pants, and white home jersey with green number 53 on it. His uniform is so clean he could be in a Tide commercial, but he's groaning in pain and his right arm is crossed over his chest.

"You know I can't raise my damn hand," Eugene says, glaring. "Look at me!"

Since he doesn't seem to be really hurt, I feel free to mock him.

"That's *righhhhht,*" I say, grinning really wide. "You

can't raise your hand. Which, ironically, *makes* you the little gingerbread boy."

"I'm the little gingerbread boy!" Eugene says. "Fine, I admit it. I'm the damn gingerbread boy!"

He's red in the face. I hope I'm aggravating that ulcer of his. Man, I'm sorry I missed all this crap last year. I *love* homecoming.

Up until Eugene's injury, the actual football game was a nonevent. I guess the Julius athletic directors were looking for a team who wouldn't beat us at our homecoming, so we're playing a team called the Farmers: two lame mascots and two lame teams.

"This is like the Olympics of incompetence," Dave said during the second quarter, after their receiver dropped a pass.

"I think it's so great," I said, stuffing my face with Dave's Cracker Jack. "It's like watching the bloopers show on ESPN."

Damian was leaning forward and analyzing all the action.

In the stands, there were girls drinking brownish-orange liquid out of Tropicana bottles. The contents were probably 4 percent Tropicana and 96 percent Captain Morgan, booze provided by Eugene. Close to halftime, we actually scored a touchdown, and everyone went berserk.

Derek started snatching Cracker Jack out of Dave's giant bag and throwing it all over the people around us, yelling, *"Ticker-tape parade! Ticker-tape parade!"*

"Stop," Dave grumbled, swatting at Derek's hand. "Stop throwing a parade. I bet there's a flag on the play."

But there wasn't a flag on the play. Down on the field, Josh, who scored the touchdown, was running toward the bench...right at Eugene, who was waiting to give him a high five.

Except Josh wasn't going for a high five. Josh was going for the chest bump. And that's when Eugene went down.

The kid went down so *hard*, I'm telling you. According to Chung, who was right there next to them, there was this *crunch* sound, like what you hear when you sit on a bag of pretzels. That was Eugene's collarbone.

So here we are. The paramedics are taking Eugene's insurance information when Josh comes jogging over.

"Oh my God, dude," Josh says, coming around the side of the stretcher with his helmet jammed under his arm. "I am *so* sorry."

"Don't worry about it," Eugene says in a dramatic, croaky voice. "It was for the good of the team."

Josh leans in toward Eugene.

"Hey, uh...Eugene?" Josh says in a low voice. "You're not gonna, like..."

"Die?" I suggest loudly, spitting a few pieces of Cracker Jack out of my mouth.

"...sue me," Josh finishes. "You're not gonna sue me, right? Because last month I smashed my dad's car, and I'm still paying off—"

"Hey, hey," Eugene interrupts. "We're teammates. We're, like, brothers."

"Italian silk," Josh says, smiling.

"Italian silk," Eugene agrees. Then he crosses his left hand over his body and extends his fist toward Josh. They fist-bump. Apparently, Eugene can fist-bump adequately. It's just the chest bump he can't handle.

Just as Josh leaves, Bobbi wobbles toward us in her dumb high-heeled shoes. It probably took her twenty minutes to climb down from the bleachers and get across this grass.

"How is he?" she asks me first, gripping my arm like we're outside an operating room together or something.

"Uh..." I'm confused, so I just gesture to Eugene. "He's...right there."

When the paramedic steps away from his side, Bobbi approaches Eugene.

"Does it hurt *so bad*?" she asks, with huge eyes.

"I'm toughing it out," Eugene replies. The croaky voice is back now.

"Do you have to go to the hospital?" Bobbi asks, looking at the ambulance, which has its back doors open.

"The emergency room," Eugene says.

I think Bobbi is actually about to cry. *Holy shit. Maybe she actually likes him.*

"Can I come with you in the ambulance?" Bobbi asks. She takes his hand.

"I don't want you to see me like this," Eugene tells her.

"Do you think you'll make it to the party at Pam's house later?" Bobbi asks.

"I might be in a cast," Eugene warns her. "But I think I'll make it."

"I'll be waiting there for you," Bobbi says. "Text me?"

"I will," Eugene says.

Then something happens that's even more mind-blowing than a touchdown by our crappy football team. Bobbi kisses Eugene. And it's not a one-second "bye" kind of kiss, either. This kiss lasts a solid five seconds.

Then the paramedics roll the stretcher away and load Eugene into the back of the ambulance. Halftime is over, so the players are back on the field. As for me, I just stand there shaking my head, eating Cracker Jack, and thinking, *Well done, little gingerbread boy.*

CHAPTER 10: KELLY

*"Is She Really Going Out with Him?
What Julius Hotties See in Grimy Guys"*

"The Boy Recession©" by Aviva Roth,
The Julius Journal, October

Five dollars," Amy Schiffer tells us at the barn door.

"We have to pay five dollars to hang out in someone's barn with a bunch of pig shit?" Darcy asks, crossing her arms over her blazer.

"It's *organic* pig shit," Amy informs her.

This is homecoming in Wisconsin. Whitefish Bay is definitely suburban—it's just north of Milwaukee—but, for some reason, whenever homecoming rolls around, we end up on the semirural outskirts of town, like all those stereotypes of the Midwest. In a good year, the party is at someone's lake house. In the worst years, everyone drinks in a field or the woods. I guess this year is in between— we're at the two-story barn in back of Pam's family's organic farm. They have a lot of property on the edge of town, and to get back here we had to walk through yards and yards of mud in our new boots.

Plus, it's freezing. I can see my breath, and Aviva is looking down her shirt, checking for goose bumps in her cleavage. Aviva pushes in front of Darcy, unzips her wallet, and asks Amy, "Do you take credit cards?"

"Seriously?" Amy says, zipping her bomber jacket up to her neck. So I take ten dollars out of my purse and hand it to Amy. The money was from my mom, who thinks that I was going to Applebee's before spending the night at Aviva's house.

"Here. That's for me and Aviva," I tell Amy. "Darce, do you have cash?"

Just then a group of freshman boys comes up behind us.

"Hey, guys!" Amy says, sounding very perky all of a sudden. "Welcome to the party! We've got a huge selection of drinks in there. There's a keg and a bunch of cups near the door, and there's a whole table of hard lemonade and local beers and stuff. Help yourselves!"

Then she opens the door, smiles, and ushers them in. The smell of Axe body spray lingers in a trail behind them.

"Excuse me!" Darcy pushes up to Amy as she's closing the barn door. "Why didn't *they* have to pay?"

Amy takes her place as barn bouncer again and crosses her arms.

"They're guys," she says.

"So what?"

"Girls have to pay to get in," Amy says. "Guys don't."

"*Those* guys?" Aviva says. "They're freshmen. And they're stinky! They're *stinky freshmen.*"

Reaching into her enormous purse, Aviva pulls out a full glass bottle of Ralph Lauren perfume. She starts spraying it in the air between Darcy and Amy.

"Beggars can't be choosers," Amy says, waving the perfume away. "In case you guys haven't heard, we're in a *boy recession.*"

"What?" I ask. I choke on Aviva's perfume. "Where did you hear that—the boy recession?"

"Eugene told Bobbi, and Bobbi told us," Amy says.

Ah. She heard it through the spandexer grapevine.

"But it's true," she adds. "You'll see when you go in there."

Inside, the barn actually looks very girly. Pam strung up these red Christmas lights on the walls to decorate it, so the whole place has a pinkish glow, and the spandexers bought a bulk case of plastic cocktail glasses, so I guess they're drinking cosmos. I have no idea what's in a cosmo, but I'm pretty sure Carrie Bradshaw never drank one in a barn while wearing UGGs.

It doesn't just look like a boy recession in here, it *sounds* like a boy recession. From a rung of the loft ladder, a pink iPod is blaring Katy Perry's "I Kissed a Girl." Pam, who obviously started drinking back when she put up those Christmas lights, is grabbing any senior she can find and announcing, "This is, seriously, our *last* homecoming!"

"You wanna play How Many Minutes 'Til She Pukes?" Darcy asks me, nodding at Pam.

This is our favorite Julius party game.

"*Hmm,* I don't know if I can do minutes," I say. "But I'll give her one and a half more Wisconsin cosmos."

Darcy, Aviva, and I veer off to the closest corner of the barn and end up by the keg. We don't drink, but a lot of people in Wisconsin do. So in order to be loyal to our state, Darcy, Aviva, and I hold red Solo cups and pretend to get into the spirit of things.

"Watch it," Derek Palewski says, seeing me looking at a bottled drink that has a label printed in Japanese. "That Tokyo Pomegranate Surprise was imported by Eugene for Bobbi only. But"—he cheers up and smiles—"you may select from any of our other delicious beverages."

"Are you the bartender?" Aviva asks him.

"I delivered all this crap," Derek says. "I work for Eugene now. He paid me in beers. You can have one of mine, if you want."

Derek holds out the can he's drinking from, and Aviva reads the label.

"*Milwaukee's Second-Best?*"

"Is that a real brand?" I ask him.

"MSB? Hell, yeah, it is," Derek says. "Official beer of slackers."

Derek tilts his head back to take a gulp and then lets out a huge burp. Darcy says, "Ew," glaring at him.

"Sorry, wife," Derek says as he comes around from behind the table to sling his arm around Darcy's shoulders.

When Derek was in freshman bio class with us, he told our teacher he had to sit out the evolution unit because his parents were evangelicals. When our teacher found out that Derek lied and the Palewskis are full-blown Darwinists, Derek was forced to catch up on the entire unit in three days. Darcy was his tutor. He promised he'd pay her back by marrying her someday.

Now, when Darcy pushes his arm off, Derek wheedles, "C'mon, we could be a power couple. You'll be president, I'll be a rock star...."

"A rock star?" Darcy raises one eyebrow. "Your band is fictional."

"Currently fictional, yes," Derek says, nodding. "But until we get our record deal, I guess I could be a stay-at-home dad."

Over at the other end of the table, Aviva is pouring us three no-rum-and-Cokes.

"Someone needs to put these freshmen in their place," she says. "I just got hit on by Axe-body-spray guy."

As Darcy takes her plastic cup from Aviva, Derek looks offended.

"President Ryan!" he says. "You'll drink that, and you won't drink my MSB?"

"No, thanks," Darcy says, and meets his eyes with a smirk. "I don't settle for the second best of anything."

"Hi, girls! Happy homecoming!"

Bobbi Novak comes skipping up to us in her tiny T-shirt, frayed denim miniskirt, and UGGs, holding a Wisconsin cosmo. She kisses each of us on the cheek.

"Darcy, are those new boots? So cute! And I wanted to tell you you're doing *such* a great job as president! Finally, some girl power!"

Aviva and I look on with amusement as Bobbi gushes to Darcy, who's trying not to roll her eyes.

"Bobbi," I say. "How's Eugene doing?"

"He's going to text me when he leaves the hospital," Bobbi says. "He had to go to the emergency room!"

"What's going on between you two?" Aviva asks.

Aviva is less subtle than I am. She loves gossip.

"Well, I guess we're just friends for now," Bobbi says with a giggle. "But he's such a great guy! He's, like, the biggest sweetheart. I never knew him that well before. I mean, last year he got me these organic hair extensions that are only available in Canada, but that was just, like, a business transaction...."

"How can hair extensions be organic?" Darcy asks.

"They take hair from someone who's on an all-organic diet," Bobbi says. Then she adds, "With their permission, of course."

"Of course."

"Eugene's just so . . . different from the guys I've been with before," Bobbi says, looking down at her phone.

Just then, Eugene comes in, sitting high on Josh's and Chung's shoulders. Once they're inside, we can see Eugene's right arm is in a sling. Hunter is behind them, holding a piece of paper and shaking his head.

"Ladies and gentlemen," Eugene calls out. *"Ladies and gentlemen!"*

A freshman girl turns down the iPod so everyone can hear Eugene. "I give you . . ." Eugene begins dramatically as he reaches down and takes the piece of paper Hunter's holding.

"My *clavicle!*"

With a flourish, he waves his X-ray, with the bones glowing pink from the red Christmas lights behind them. A huge rush of applause goes up, and Bobbi emerges from the crowd, streaking through like a comet with a fake blond extension for a tail. As soon as Eugene gets down from his human throne, she jumps on him and starts to make out with him.

"Ew, look at his tongue. He's like a snake," Aviva says, sipping her no-rum-and-Coke.

"The way people react to football players is beyond ridiculous. What would they do if the team had actually *won* the game?" Darcy asks.

"They would take their tops off," Aviva says. "Or at least unbutton a few buttons."

I hate to give pervy Eugene credit, but after those guys arrive, the party changes. Before, we were separate people in a cold space. Now everyone's all pressed together, warm and touching, sharing breath and body heat. Girls are getting wild and unwinding their scarves, and all the people bumping into me makes me feel like I'm actually drunk. At one point, I see Hunter sitting on the loft ladder, next to the iPod speakers. His neck is flushed red, and he doesn't seem to notice that Diva Price is standing next to him. I glance away for a second, and when I look back, Diva is on his lap. He looks as startled by the sudden movement as I am — did she fall on top of him? But then Hunter shrugs and relaxes, even though Diva's got her arm around his shoulders.

I usually don't think about Diva too much, but right now, her thick thighs are making me irrationally mad. Why would you wear see-through tights when your thighs are that big? And her skirt is way too short. Then I look at Hunter and feel a familiar tug when I see his hand on her shoulder. I guess I've been watching his drum lessons and I've gotten to know his long, careful musician's fingers. When he taught the kids to hold drumsticks, he told them, "You gotta let your hands be loose. Nice and easy." And even though Hunter isn't playing the drums right now, that's the right phrase for him: *nice and easy.*

"You think she's gonna eat him alive?" Aviva asks, watching the scene unfold between Diva and Hunter.

"I love him," I blurt out.

"What?" Darcy's blue eyes are huge.

"You *love* him?" Aviva sounds skeptical.

"Okay, no, no," I say. "I don't love him. I just don't know how to announce something like that. I only see this kinda stuff in romantic comedies."

"You *like* him," Aviva says, as though she's correcting my grammar.

"Yes," I say miserably.

"You like *Hairface* Hunter?" Darcy says.

"I like him," I repeat, hopelessly.

The three of us are standing and watching as Diva brushes Hunter's hair back from his face.

"Push her off," Aviva says to me. "Push her off his lap."

"I can't push her off!"

Aviva and Darcy start coming up with other plots, but I feel helpless, standing there hoping that she doesn't kiss him. *Please, don't let her kiss him.*

CHAPTER 11: HUNTER

"Halloween Costume Roundup: Could Pirate
Dave Have at Least Tried to Be Creative?"

"The Boy Recession©" by Aviva Roth,
The Julius Journal, October

You got in late last night!" my mom says when she comes
into my room.

It's 3 PM on the Saturday after homecoming, and I'm
still in bed. I'm actually awake — I'm sitting up against the
wall with my guitar on my stomach, picking out chords —
but I'm still in bed. I love my bed so much that sometimes I
stay in it for a whole weekend.

Most moms would probably be pissed if they came into
their son's room and he was lazing under a pile of crap that
included an open package of those orange peanut-butter
crackers. Not my mom. She also doesn't mind that I was
out 'til 1 AM last night, when Dave, who was angry about
being designated driver for the homecoming party, literally
pushed me out of his slow-moving car and onto my lawn.
All she says when she sits down on my super-comfortable

broken-down mattress is: "I'm glad you could sleep in this morning! You need it. How was the game last night?"

She reaches over and brushes my hair out of my eyes.

"Good," I tell her, yawning and dropping my guitar pick onto my blanket. "Eugene got hurt, but he'll be okay."

"He got to play in the game?" my mom says. "Good for him!"

"Nah. Actually," I say, "it was kind of a...warm-up injury. I don't know if he'll ever get to play."

"I'm sure he will," my mom says. "He needs time to learn the game. He'll get his chance."

My mom is used to underdogs from her job with the Milwaukee public school system, where she does art therapy with "problem kids." That sounds pretty depressing, but my mom is good at it, and the kids like her. She's big into self-expression, so her students get to decide on their own projects. This one kid who stabbed someone in a fight started working with my mom on a Jackson Pollock project, where he would go in a room and throw paint around and make these gigantic, crazy paintings. He got so into it that he started bringing paintbrushes to school instead of knives.

Her teaching style — valuing self-expression and personal freedom — definitely shows up in her parenting, too. When I was growing up, she would let me wear whatever I wanted. I could wear my Halloween costume to school and refuse to cut my hair for four years, and she was cool with it.

When I get my pick and start playing the guitar again, my mom watches me for a few minutes, smiling.

"Did you write that one?" she asks.

"Yeah. I'm starting a song," I tell her. "I never finish them, though."

"I have a bunch of staff paper downstairs that I took from the school," my mom says. "You should write down what you've written so far!"

"Yeah. I have to figure this part out first," I say. "I keep messing it up."

"Well, I stole a lot of paper," my mom says, winking, and then whispers, "*So you can make lots of mistakes.*"

My mom gives me a hug, which is really brave, because I haven't showered and I still smell like Dave's car. She doesn't seem to mind. Then she gets up, and as she pulls the door shut behind her, she says, "There's bacon downstairs, too."

Half an hour later, I'm still in bed. The only thing that's changed is that a pile of blank staff paper and a plate of bacon crumbs are in bed with me. I'm still leaning against the wall, picking at my guitar, when my dad comes bursting into my room.

"Let's get going!" he says, clapping his hands. His clap is so loud it hurts my ears. "Let's go and get a pumpkin."

"What?" I yawn at him. "When is Halloween? Soon?"

"Halloween is next week!"

Whoa. Seriously?

"We've gotta get ready," my dad is saying. "We've gotta stock up on candy, we've gotta put the spiderwebs out on the bushes, get the fog machine out.... What if we did a haunted-house thing this year? Whadda you think about that? You and I could hide in the bushes, and when kids come out, we'll jump out...."

This plan sounds like something we could get sued for. Plus, I'm not sure I want to spend Halloween night hiding out in a bush with my dad, waiting to jump out and make little kids cry. I've gotta go out with Derek and six cans of shaving cream and make bigger people cry. But for now, to make my dad happy, I'll go get a pumpkin.

Let me give you some advice here: People who want to have the sex talk with you will act the same way as people who want to murder you. First they get you in their car, so they're in control and you can't escape. Then they drive you someplace in the middle of nowhere. Today my dad takes me to a farm on the outskirts of Whitefish Bay. On the hunt for one of those huge monster pumpkins they inject steroids into, my dad treks farther and farther back in the field, back where there's a lot of wet grass and mud and animal shit, and my sneakers are sinking into the ground. When we're back in the last few rows of pumpkins —

this is the isolation thing I'm talking about—my dad says, "So I saw Gene Pluskota at the hardware store this morning. He said Eugene has a girlfriend!"

Wow. Eugene works fast. When did he tell his dad about Bobbi? It had to be sometime between midnight last night, when they stopped making out long enough to agree that they were actually dating, and 9 AM, when my dad was at the hardware store.

"So..." my dad follows up, grunting as he rolls this huge pumpkin over. No go. It's all rotten on the back side. "Anything going on with you in that department?"

Crap. Well, I guess he had to ask about my love life eventually. But I don't have a lot to tell him. Some people think Eugene and I are dating, because we're always together and he pays for my food. I do hook up with girls, but my hook-ups are pretty sketchy. Usually I'm drunk or the girl's drunk, or she's pissed at another dude who rejected her, and we're in some weird location. Once I made out with a girl in Dave's smelly parked car in the Applebee's parking lot. Maybe it means something that girls kiss me only in dark places. I tell my dad, "Uh, not too much going on."

I go over to this huge pumpkin and try to check out the bottom side.

"Well, I think your stock is up," my dad tells me. "I think you're growing into your looks," he continues.

Uh... What? Seriously, Dad? What is that, the consolation prize of compliments?

My dad's comment does remind me of something Eugene said last night, though. When we were waiting for his X-rays, he told me Bobbi's friends have been talking about me. "Some of them are hot for you, Huntro," he told me. "They said your hair was cute." Then he corrected himself. "Well, they called it 'messy cute.'"

I didn't know if "messy cute" was good or bad, and I didn't really believe Eugene anyway, but then later at the party, Diva Price sat on my lap. Diva is one of Bobbi's friends, and she's kind of loud, but she's not too bad-looking.

I didn't hook up with her, though. I had just chugged a beer, and I was still walking that tightrope between puking and not puking.

"...So if you ever need any advice," my dad is saying, "you know the guy to come to. I think I had some moves, back in the day...."

Then my dad goes off on some tangent and ends up talking about the guy from the Old Spice commercials, and I realize that my dad's not going to murder me or give me the sex talk. He just wants to bond. My dad's been really into bonding with me since he lost his job. I think it makes him feel like he's doing something. Like, even if he's not making any progress finding a job, at least he's getting some quality time with his son. Walking through the pumpkin patch, I find the biggest one in the back row and roll it all around to make sure it looks good. Then I point it out to my dad, who picks it up by himself, which is impressive.

"Wow, yeah, this one looks good!" he says. I grab the other side, and we start backing up. It's a long-ass way back to the table where you pay for stuff, and my arms hurt already.

"You know what we need?" he says. "Did you see, on the table, those huge carving knives? We should go crazy with carving this year...."

My dad needs to find a job soon, because I need a break from the quality time. I can't lift stuff like this anymore.

CHAPTER 12: KELLY

"Gold-Digger Guys: Warning Signs"

"The Boy Recession©" by Aviva Roth,
The Julius Journal, November

Kelly! Hey, Kelly!"

The last class bell just rang, and Bobbi Novak is chasing me down the hallway, her heels clicking and squeaking against the tile floor. I turn around to talk to her, mostly because I want to get close enough to check out her necklace, a sparkling light blue stone dangling from a thin gold chain resting in the deep chasm of Bobbi's cleavage. The much-talked-about necklace is a gift from Eugene, who is now officially Bobbi's boyfriend. Her Facebook profile picture is the two of them, taken last week, when they dressed up as Hugh Hefner and a Playboy Bunny for Halloween.

"I'm organizing Open-Mic Night this year, and I'd love you to be part of it!" Bobbi says.

"Oh, I'm definitely coming. Aviva and Darcy and I go every year."

"Actually, I was hoping you would perform!" Bobbi says. "You're so amazing on the flute, and everyone would love it if you'd play something!"

I seriously doubt that. I can't imagine getting up on the Julius stage on a Friday night and serenading a rowdy, half-drunk audience with a Mozart aria.

"Maybe next year," I say. "Have you asked Amy to perform? She's an amazing dancer."

"I have her name right here!" Bobbi says, pointing to her clipboard. "She's leading our new stomp group. I'm so excited to watch them! But you should—"

"Sorry, I've gotta run in here and get something! Sorry!" I say, cutting Bobbi off. I back up against the band room's door and escape inside.

When I go to the cubby to take out my flute, I see Hunter. He's sitting on the first level of the bandstand. I've noticed that he almost never sits on chairs—he spends most of his time in this room balanced up on the railings of the bandstand, swinging his legs, or sometimes he'll hop up onto the closed lid of the grand piano, except when Johann is around. Even though he's younger than us, Johann makes both Hunter and me want to behave ourselves. Right now Hunter's playing a few chords on his guitar, stopping and starting the same chords over again. It's been less than a week since I realized that I like Hunter, and now I find him alone, looking cute. Maybe Aviva's right, and the universe wants us to be together.

"Hey," I say.

Hunter starts and drops his guitar pick. When he turns around and sees me, a slow smile comes across his face.

"Hey!" he says. "What are you up to?"

I grab one of Johann's music theory textbooks off the piano before sitting down on the bandstand next to Hunter.

"I thought I'd brush up on my dotted quarter notes and sforzandos," I tell him. "I think Johann's teaching my kids so much that they know more than me now."

"Seriously! That kid is intense. He knows so much. He explained to my kids how Beethoven wrote music when he was deaf! It blew my mind!" Hunter says with a laugh.

"And he can play every instrument!" I add, opening my flute case on my lap and starting to twist the head-piece in.

"You know those one-man bands, where the guy has the harmonica in his mouth and the drum kit strapped to his back? I think Johann could be one of those," I say.

"No way," he says. "Not in those khakis. He's too serious! I mean, he's fifteen, and my kids call him 'Mr. Johann.'"

I bring the flute to my mouth, test out a note, and then lower it to pull the headpiece out, which changes the pitch.

"Is it really that hard to make a sound on that thing?" he asks me. "All your little flute girls are always huffin' and puffin' over there."

"It's harder than it looks," I tell him, adding, with mock arrogance, "I've got mad skills."

"Oh, yeah?" Hunter says, tilting his head and grinning at me.

"You think you can do it?"

"Well, I'm no one-man band, but I think I can handle it."

When I give him the flute, our hands overlap for a second. Hunter puts his fingers in the wrong place, but he blows a pretty decent note.

"Not bad, Fahrenbach," I say. "But what can you play on that thing?"

I'm looking at the guitar.

"Uh, well, I can play anything, kind of," Hunter says. "I mean, I just listen to stuff, and I play it back. Beatles, Hendrix, Clapton, whatever. Acoustic stuff, Ani DiFranco..."

"You play Ani DiFranco songs?" I say, staring at him. "You know who Ani DiFranco *is*?"

"Hell, yeah," Hunter says. "I listen to everything. What, you don't think I'm a fan of, like, bisexual feminist folk songs?"

"You've got hidden depths."

"When you rock, you rock, Robbins," Hunter says. "Nah, but mostly I play your basic Stoner's Greatest Hits. Ya know, 'Wonderwall' by Oasis, 'Ants Marching' by Dave Matthews Band, 'The General' by Dispatch..."

Hunter starts with "Wonderwall," but then, as he's playing, the melody changes and all of a sudden he's playing "Ants Marching." Then "Ants Marching" slows down into the chorus of "The General." Then it all flows into another Oasis song I can't remember the name of. It's amazing—Hunter's finding the exact right notes and chords that let one song in one musical key meld into a different song in a different musical key.

"Did you *write* that?" I ask him, so impressed.

"That?" Hunter picks out a few notes of the last song. "That's 'Champagne Supernova.' That's Oasis."

"No, the whole thing. The medley. Did you write the medley?"

"Oh!" Hunter shrugs. "I'm just playing all the songs I know, basically. They work together. You know, something like this..."

And he starts playing and singing a song I love—"Crash into Me" by Dave Matthews Band. He's singing it the same hoarse way Dave Matthews sings it, and his voice is really good. He transitions from "Crash Into Me" back to "Champagne Supernova," then trails off.

"Yeah, so, enough of that," Hunter says. "It's awkward with the words, 'cause I'll be singing about love or whatever and then suddenly I'm talking about people getting high."

"No! You're good!" I insist, leaning toward him. "You're seriously good."

"*Nahhhhh*," Hunter drawls, relaxing his legs, which lowers his guitar.

"Yes! You can really sing. I had no clue."

"I just sing," Hunter says, shrugging. "I dunno."

"You're actually talented!"

That sounds terrible, so we both laugh as soon as I say it.

"I write some stuff, too," Hunter says.

"You write *songs*?" My voice is even squeakier and more ridiculous.

"Well, no, not songs," Hunter says. "I start songs, but I never finish them. I just write, like, four bars of music, and then I play it over and over."

"Did you write what you were playing when I came in?" I ask. "I wanna hear it!"

After I pester him, Hunter plays a verse of a song that's really, really good.

"I get stuck after that last chord," Hunter says.

"Here, play the end for me again."

We're sitting so close that my leg is right next to his guitar, and it feels cozy, even though we're in a big empty room.

"What about a G chord next?" I suggest. Then, after he plays it, "No, that's not what I'm thinking. Try a G seventh?"

A half-hour goes by, and the song is coming together. I'm giving Hunter suggestions and listening to him try things out until we have three verses and a chorus figured out.

"That's a cool sound right there," Hunter says, playing a transition. "Yeah — I like that shift, the way it changes."

"So that's the whole thing, the whole song," I say. "Play it from the beginning!"

As he plays, Hunter hums, and I wonder if he's already

thinking of words for the verses. At the end, he plays the chorus twice.

When he's done, I'm so amazed that I blurt out, "Someone should hear you!"

The guitar strings are still vibrating, so Hunter covers them with his hand to still them, looks up, and says, "You are someone."

My face and neck feel hot. Under all his messy hair, Hunter's eyes are intensely fixed on me, but I can't hold his gaze too long. I stand up and walk to the piano to return the theory book that I never opened.

"Have you heard about this thing Bobbi is doing?" I ask him. "The Open-Mic Night?"

"I think Eugene told me something about it. What is it?"

"It's kinda like a talent show. You just get up, sing one song, and that's it. You should sign up!"

"I don't know," Hunter says, absentmindedly moving his fingers up and down the guitar strings.

"Come on. You should do it."

"I'd have to write words and everything," Hunter says, looking up at me from the bandstand.

"You can write lyrics. That's the easy part. You wrote a whole song! You can write lyrics."

In a gesture of confidence, I hop up onto the piano and swing my feet in the same way Hunter always does. He grins.

"Well, Ms. Duff does say I've got some verbal skills," he says. "Even though I use the word 'crap' way too much."

"See! I agree with her! You should do it. You should
totally do it."

Hunter takes his guitar off and rests it next to him.
Without it, he seems kind of vulnerable, like it was a shield
or something. He leans forward. "You think I should?"

"I'm making you," I tell him, smiling.

Hunter throws his head back and makes a playful
growling sound, like he's frustrated, but when he leans forward again, he's smiling. He's made up his mind.

"So how long do I have to write this thing?" he asks.

"Two weeks."

"Two weeks?" He sighs.

I slide down from the piano and go back over to the
bandstand. Resting my hand on his guitar, wishing it was
his arm or leg, I tell him, "I have complete faith in you."

CHAPTER 13: HUNTER

"Unlikely Heartthrobs:
The Shy Guy, the Slacker, and the Video Game God"

"The Boy Recession©" by Aviva Roth,
The Julius Journal, November

Dude, are ulcers contagious?" I ask Eugene. "I think you gave me yours."

Eugene's had an ulcer since eighth grade. The stress of running his business and freaking out about getting busted, plus the huge cups of black coffee he drinks every morning, have eaten a hole in his stomach. I don't know what an ulcer feels like, but right now, my stomach feels weird, like there's a bunch of battery acid sloshing around in there. I'm backstage in the Julius auditorium, and all the people who are going to perform in this open-mic thing tonight are crammed backstage.

Eugene ignores my question and walks over to the curtain so that he can watch Bobbi onstage.

"Look at her out there," he says. "How amazing is my girlfriend?"

Bobbi's the MC tonight, so she's giving a little speech about whatever disease we're raising money for before introducing the next act.

"My girlfriend put this whole thing together," Eugene says. "She's incredible! She did all the publicity; she got all these people here. Look at this, Huntro—the place is packed!"

"Is it really?" I ask.

I go up to the curtain and look out. *Damn.* All the seats are full, and some people are standing in the aisles, too.

I groan loudly and clutch at my stomach again.

"What's going on with you?" Eugene asks, turning around.

"My stomach."

"What'd you eat tonight?"

"Uh…a bacon cheeseburger. Three Fruit Roll-Ups. Some chili out of a can without heating it up."

"Okay, so the usual," Eugene says. He grabs my face with both of his hands and squishes it. I hate when he does this. He stares at me for a creepy length of time, then gives his diagnosis. "You are *stressed*," he pronounces.

He's more excited about this than the big audience is. I pull away from him and pick at my guitar, trying to tune it. But my fingers are acting weird, so I'm just plucking random strings.

"You are *stressed out*," Eugene repeats, totally pumped. "That's what's wrong with your stomach! You are *stressed*."

He points his finger in my face, and I reach up to slap it away.

"Shut up, dude," I tell him. "I don't get stressed. *You* get stressed."

Eugene laughs, all gleeful and evil.

"I don't stress!" I repeat, starting to get heated. "I fell asleep during a final last year."

"Because you didn't give a crap about that," Eugene says. "But you give a crap about this."

My stomach is still churning. I groan again. Eugene reaches into his pocket and hands me a plastic wrapper with pink pills in it.

"Pepto-Bismol," he tells me. "I'm always packing."

Onstage, Bobbi is talking to the audience. "Our next act is really exciting, you guys. With their debut performance, Julius P. Heil High School's one and only stomp team—White Kid Stomp!"

Kids in red jumpsuits start pushing past me, which doesn't help my stomach.

When the stomp kids start stomping and clapping, Bobbi comes backstage and immediately runs up to Eugene.

"Hi, baby!" she says. "I didn't know you were back here!"

Eugene grabs her and kisses her. When they disentangle, Bobbi turns to me and says, "You're on after Diva, and Diva's on next. Do you see her? Diva! Oh my gosh, you look amazing!"

Jesus. Diva just came out of one of the dressing rooms wearing some crazy short dress that looks like a disco ball.

"Hi, Hunter. How are you?" Diva says, smiling at me and putting her hand on my arm. Bobbi said Diva looks amazing, but I don't see it. Usually she's okay-looking—tall and kinda thick for a girl, with brown hair, brown eyes, and orange skin because she uses that fake-tanning crap—but tonight she put all this makeup on top of her orange skin, and there are way too many colors going on on her face.

"Uhh, okay," I say.

"You can have my dressing room if you want," she says. "So you can change."

What? Why would I need to change? I'm wearing socks and shoes and jeans and a red T-shirt that says: *Got Crabs? Maryland.* I'm even wearing deodorant.

When I look up from my shirt, Diva is sticking out her face. *What is she doing?*

"Give me a kiss for luck!" she says.

I quickly kiss her cheek and then look for an excuse to run away.

"Uh...I've got to...uh...I have to tune my guitar!" I say, and quickly walk farther backstage, where Johann is organizing sheet music and wearing a dress shirt. *Is that what Diva meant when she said I should change?*

"Yo, Johann!" I call out. "What's up? You playing the piccolo tonight?" I ask him.

"No, I'm accompanying people on the piano," he says, holding up his sheet music.

"Cool," I say.

"What are you playing tonight?" Johann asks me.

"Something I wrote," I say. "It's kind of...I don't know. Acoustic stuff. Just a song."

Johann's looking at me like I'm an idiot, but then he offers to help tune my guitar. I have a pretty good sense of when the notes are right, but Johann's amazing. He takes charge and tells me exactly which strings to tighten and by how much.

"Damn," I tell him. "You're good at this shit!"

"I have perfect pitch," he says.

We finish tuning just in time to hear Diva belting out a high note in the song she's singing. Or trying to belt it. I give Johann this look, like, *What the hell?*

"She's flat," he tells me. "Very, very flat."

"Man," I say, whistling. "I don't wanna go out there and sing, but if I don't go out there, she'll never shut up."

"You don't want to sing?" Johann asks.

"I dunno," I say. "I think I've got this stomach thing...."

"It could be performance anxiety."

A normal person would say "stage fright." But freakin' Johann and his khakis have to make it sound like I need Viagra or something.

"If you don't want to sing, why did you sign up?" Johann asks.

Valid question. The first answer that pops into my head is: It seemed like a good idea at the time. But the real answer probably has something to do with Kelly. I've been thinking about her all the time. Lately, when I zone out in class, I've been picturing one specific thing about her — like those crinkles she gets around her eyes when she smiles, or the freckles around her nose that I noticed even though they're almost invisible. Or I'll remember something she said or how she reached out and touched my arm. She does that to people a lot, and she doesn't even notice she's doing it — but I notice.

Usually I don't even bother liking girls, but with Kelly I can't help it. And when Diva stops singing, Kelly pops into my head again. I forget about my ulcer because I'm busy hoping she's out there rooting for me.

CHAPTER 14: KELLY

"It's Raining Women:
Female Performers Make Up 80 Percent of
Open-Mic Night Performance"

"The Boy Recession©" by Aviva Roth,
The Julius Journal, November

How would you describe his outfit?" Aviva whispers to me and Darcy.

Leaning across me, Darcy whispers back, "Gas-station casual."

She's talking about Hunter, so I hit her.

"Don't be mean, Darce," I say. "It's hard to get up onstage. It doesn't matter what he's wearing. And no one made fun of you when you wore a power tie to the first day of kindergarten."

Darcy, Aviva, and I are in the second row of the Julius auditorium, front and center. Surprisingly, Aviva's the one who got here early and snagged us our seats—she's covering the event for the school newspaper.

The spotlights on the stage must be strong, because when Hunter comes out onstage, he squints and raises his hand to shield his eyes. I don't care what Darcy says about his clothes; I think Hunter looks cute in his baggy jeans, Chuck Taylors, and red shirt. I think his shirt says something about crabs on it, but when he slips the strap of his guitar over his head, the guitar covers the shirt. Plus, he looks really, really good holding the guitar.

"This is the song he played for you?" Darcy asks me.

I told Darcy and Aviva all about the universe bringing me and Hunter together in the band room.

"Yeah. He played part of it for me, and I helped him with the chorus."

"You wrote it *together*?" Darcy asks. "You're, like, a musical power couple!"

"You wrote it together?" Aviva repeats, and starts scribbling in her notebook.

"Stop!" I tell her. "Don't write that! I just gave him some ideas. He wrote it himself. I haven't even heard the words yet."

"The melody was a collaboration with celebrated Julius High School flautist Kelly Robbins. . . ." Aviva narrates as she writes.

"Stop it!" I say, and look back to the stage.

"Hey," Hunter says into the microphone.

Then he squints into the audience again. *Can he see me? Or are the lights too bright?* He sort of waves at the audience, and Aviva whispers, "Awkward wave," and makes a note on her notepad.

I snatch her pen out of her hand.

"Okay, so, uh, thanks for being here and, uh, paying five bucks," Hunter says into the microphone. "Hopefully we, um, cure that disease. So! Here's my song. And it doesn't have a name, so..."

I'm not sure what other people expect from Hunter. I mean, no one's ever heard him sing before. So when he starts playing, I get nervous for him. I actually close my eyes and hold my breath for the first few measures of him strumming the guitar. Then he starts to sing.

> *Sure, of course, terrain is rough*
> *My aching arms are not enough*
> *You're the healer, I'm the holder,*
> *But the world turns darker, colder*

I open my eyes and smile. He can sing. And he can write, too! The lyrics are so...sweet. And smart. This is a real song. When I hear the chords leading into the chorus, I think, *I helped him write this!* I would never let Aviva print it in the newspaper, but I did help.

> *You're the soft place that I fall*
> *After all*
> *Every everyday disaster*
> *The days of running farther, faster*
> *Fall down here with me*

As he moves into the second verse, Hunter seems more comfortable onstage.

You know my shape, and let me sink
And see my strength, and give me lift
And they don't know, no, they don't see
The me when you're alone with me

As soon as the song ends, Darcy turns to me, fixes her blue eyes on me, and says, "Oh. My. God."

Around us, everyone is clapping and the sophomore girls next to me are saying, "Aw!" In the aisle near us, Damian is cheering and Derek is yelling, "Huntro! Huntro!" in his hoarse voice. The seniors in the front row stand up to give Hunter a standing ovation, and I stand, too, partly because Hunter deserves it and partly because they're blocking my view.

Aviva whips out her digital camera, scurries down the aisle, and crouches next to the orchestra pit to point her camera up at Hunter. He does another awkward-yet-adorable wave and then walks offstage. Even though his head is down, I can tell he's still smiling.

"He's good, right?" I say to Darcy when I sit down.

She doesn't even answer. She turns to face me and grips the armrest between us with both of her hands.

"That song was about you!" she says.

"What?"

"Did you hear the lyrics?" Darcy says. "That thing

about giving him strength or whatever…You're the one who realized he could sing. And you gave him strength by telling him about the Open-Mic Night. *'When you're alone with me…'* You helped him write when you guys were alone in the band room. And the chorus! I mean, *'You're the soft place that I fall….'* He's talking about someone he's really comfortable with. That's what the whole thing is about. And you're the first person he felt *comfortable* singing in front of."

"That was some pretty quick analysis, Darce. I don't know," I say. "No wonder you bolted out of the AP lit exam after one hour."

"I had to pee, so I rushed the last essay. But I still got a five," Darcy informs me. "But seriously, Kelly! The song!"

It's intermission, and the auditorium lights come on. Darcy and I stand up to let the sophomore girls get out of our row. When we sit down, I tell Darcy, "You can just write a song to write a song. Songs don't always have to be *about* someone."

Aviva hurries up from the orchestra pit, frantically flipping the sheets of her yellow notepad.

"Everyone's trying to figure out who the song's about," Aviva reports, out of breath. As soon as she sits down, she starts scribbling messy notes.

"I told you it was about someone!" Darcy tells me. "You can tell by the way he sang it."

"What do you mean?"

"He was so…emotional," Darcy explains, sounding

awed. "I mean, think about Hunter Fahrenbach in class. He just, like, sits there, huffing Sharpies. But tonight he was . . . *deep*."

"Pam thinks it was about a fat girl," Aviva says, not even looking up as she fills the last line of her notepad.

"What?"

"Because it goes" — Aviva removes the pen from her mouth and uses it to flip her yellow pages back to where she jotted down lyrics — "*'You're the soft place that I fall.'*"

"Oh, that is so dumb, Pam," Darcy says, rolling her eyes. "It's a *metaphorical* soft place. It's a comfortable place. It's a supportive place. Or a supportive person. It's Kelly!"

"It's Kelly?" Aviva says, her voice going an octave higher than usual. Then she looks up, confused. "But Kelly's not fat."

"Stop!" I say. "It's not about me. It's definitely not about me."

But part of me wants them to keep saying that it *is* about me.

"I never see Hunter with any other girl," Darcy says.

"Except Diva Price," I suggest miserably. "Remember homecoming?"

"That wouldn't be a soft place to fall." Aviva snorts. "That girl is built like Michael Vick."

"Diva sat in his lap, but they didn't actually talk to each other," Darcy says. "The only other person Hunter talks to is pervy Eugene. So unless the song is about Eugene, it's about you."

I look from Darcy to Aviva. They're both completely convinced.

"Okay, okay!" I say. "What do I do about it?"

The lights in the auditorium are flashing on and off, which makes me feel like time is running out.

"Go backstage!" Darcy tells me.

"What do I do?" I ask them frantically as the lights flash for the last time. "I mean, what do I say? I can't just go up and ask who the song was about!"

Aviva doesn't answer, because she's trying to push my boobs up.

"That's as high as they go," I tell her, and she looks disappointed.

"Stop that!" Darcy slaps Aviva's hand away. "Kell, congratulate him. Tell him you loved the song. Then he might—"

"No." Aviva shakes her head. "You won't even have to say anything! He's gonna make out with you."

The lights go out, and I hurry up the darkened auditorium aisle. But backstage, things don't go so well. The wings are so crowded, it takes me a minute to even spot Hunter, who looks ridiculously good wearing a guitar... and hanging out with freshman girls. They're freshman twins who did a mime act during the first half of the show. They still have their white mime makeup all over their faces and hands, and it's rubbing off on the water bottles they're holding. Their mime act was totally bizarre, and not very good—Aviva reviewed it as "Not even the best miming I've seen in Whitefish Bay," which is pretty sad.

But it looks like they're pretty entertaining right now, because Hunter is laughing loudly at something one of them said. Then he stands up, takes his guitar off, and puts it around one of the girls' necks. He starts showing her where to put her fingers to play a chord.

My forward momentum fades away. I stop where I am, half hidden by a drum set. Suddenly I feel stupid for believing Darcy and Aviva. If Hunter wrote a song about me, wouldn't he want to know what I thought of it? Wouldn't he be looking for me? Or at least looking around? But he's not. For a minute I thought my life was romantic and a guy wrote a song about me. Now I realize that my life isn't exciting or romantic—my life consists of hiding behind a drum set and getting overshadowed by two mimes.

CHAPTER 15: HUNTER

"Senior Girls Lobby to Take Over, Convert to Lounge Boys' Bathroom in South Hallway"

"The Boy Recession©" by Aviva Roth,
The Julius Journal, November

It's November in Wisconsin and I'm in a T-shirt, trying to rush into school, but Amy and Pam stop me before I get inside the building. Usually before school they like to sit on a bench, smoking and insulting people's clothes. I'm pretty sure you're not supposed to smoke outside school, but I guess it would be pretty hypocritical for Dr. Nicotine to say anything about it. Or maybe he's scared of Pam, like everyone else is. I usually ignore her and Amy, but today they stop me.

"We need to talk to you, Hunter," Pam says.

"We have a request," Amy adds.

Gross. Pam and Amy are blowing cigarette smoke in my face, and it smells like ass. Do girls seriously think smoking makes them look hot?

"We heard you sing at Open-Mic Night," Pam tells me.

"And we love your voice," Amy says.

"Oh! Well, cool, thanks."

"We want you to try out for the musical," Pam says.

"The what?"

"The school musical," Pam says. "The play. Didn't you see *The Music Man* last year?"

No. But since Pam's holding a lit cigarette four inches from my eye, I say, "Oh, uh, yeah. It was good."

"I'm the choreographer this year," Amy says. "And I'll probably be a lead."

"I'm in charge of costumes," Pam says. "And I'll probably be a lead, too."

Behind Pam's back, Amy shakes her head no. Pam doesn't notice because she keeps talking.

"So we don't want the show to suck. And we need boys who can actually sing, because Brad's gone."

Oh, right. Now I remember the school shows. This kid Brad Farina was always the star of them; last year, in *The Music Man*, he was the Music Man.

"I dunno," I tell them. "I can't act or anything."

"Well, the other guys trying out can't act *or* sing," Pam says. "So you've got a leg up on those losers."

Amy's cigarette has gone out, and she gives up on trying to relight it. "Please, Hunter," she begs, playing the good cop. "We really, really need you."

"Well, I dunno," I say, exhaling. *Damn.* I can see my breath. "What show is it?"

"*Chicago!*" Amy says brightly.

"Like, as in Chicago the band?" I ask. I know a few Chicago songs on the guitar.

"No," Pam says. "It's about women who murder men who deserve it."

Pam and Amy asking me to try out for the show wasn't the only weird thing to happen to me this week. The other day, in U.S. history, a girl asked to borrow a pen. From *me*. No one has ever asked to borrow a pen from me before. Girls have been touching me, too, bumping into me in the hallways and smiling afterward. Now I know what the flirtation is about: my voice. I'm like a dude version of one of those Sirens from *The Odyssey*, which we got assigned sophomore year.

I know I don't seem like a musical-theater guy, but it was a pretty nice ego boost to hear that I'm a good singer and to hear that Pam and Amy "need" me. So I decided to go for it and try out this afternoon. It's better than having Ms. Duff lecture me on what a huge disappointment I am.

So far, there are four guys here for the audition: me, Chung, a freshman whose balls haven't dropped yet, and this other weird freshman, George, who used to be in spelling bees or boy pageants or some crap.

As we stand there onstage, I turn to Chung and ask, "Did Pam put a gun to your head about this shit, too?"

"What? Nah," he says. "I like musicals! Who are you trying out for?"

"Amos."

"Who?"

"Roxie's husband, who doesn't know she's cheating on him. Ya know, he sings that 'Mr. Cellophane' song about how everyone ignores him?" I say. I had rented the *Chicago* movie from Netflix earlier in the week to figure out what the story was about. It's actually a pretty good show.

"Oh," Chung says, nodding. "In the movie, he's the guy from *Step Brothers*."

"Exactly. Amy and Pam want me to sing, but I can't act, and Amos just kinda stands there, so I won't have to do that much acting."

"All right, young men! Are we ready?" Mrs. Martin calls up from the orchestra pit.

Mrs. Martin is the oldest teacher at our school, and there's a rumor she got her job by banging Julius P. Heil himself.

"Okay, we will begin with those auditioning for the role of Billy Flynn," Mrs. Martin says. "All my Billy Flynns, please step forward."

Billy Flynn is the male lead. He's the defense lawyer with sketchy ethics, and he's always wearing suits. Basically, he's a good-looking version of Eugene.

It's a killer part, but only George steps up for the role.

"Only one Billy Flynn?" Mrs. Martin says. "All right, let's hear it."

George starts to sing and strut all across the stage, spreading his arms, pointing at random people in the audience, and belting the notes so loudly that you can hear them in the back seats of the auditorium.

He's also totally off-key.

After the first verse and chorus, Mrs. Martin calls from the orchestra pit, "Stop! Stop! Stop! Look at the music! We're in the key of C!"

"What?" George says.

"Look at the music!"

"I can't read music," George says, waving the score. "I'm just looking at the words."

"You can't read music? Get back in line," Mrs. Martin growls. "Who can read music? Young men, who can read music? None of you?"

"Uh…" Squinting down at Mrs. Martin, I raise my hand halfway. "I read music. But I want to play Amos, so…"

"I'll tell you who you will play," Mrs. Martin says. "Take the music."

She gives me a few minutes to look over "Razzle Dazzle." The song is a piece of cake. So I sing it.

After two verses, I figure that's enough, and I stop. "Oh my God!" Mrs. Martin says to the piano player. "He did the *staccatos*! He did the *crescendos*!"

Okay, she liked it. That's good news. But George's gotta be pissed off, and he's standing behind me.

"You have a *magnificent* voice!" Mrs. Martin tells me.

"I told you!" Amy calls to Mrs. Martin, popping her head out from behind the stage curtain.

"No, *I* told you," Pam corrects her, popping her head out, too.

But Mrs. Martin ignores them.

"You are my star!" she tells me. "You are the silver-tongued lion of the law, Billy Flynn!"

Silver-tongued? Definitely not me.

"I dunno about Billy Flynn," I tell Mrs. Martin, shading my eyes from the spotlights. "What about Amos? Is he still available?"

"You're not changing my mind," says Mrs. Martin. "I've found my Billy Flynn!"

CHAPTER 16: KELLY

"Girls Go Gaga for Gas Station Gang:
Saturday Sees Record Crowd Outside Shell Station"

"The Boy Recession©" by Aviva Roth,
The Julius Journal, November

Aviva has the worst parking spot at Julius, and today, as we walk the mile from her car to the school, we're huddling against each other to keep the freezing November wind off us, and I'm really regretting wearing a skirt.

"Is that Derek's car?" Aviva asks through chattering teeth.

Aviva points toward the first two rows of spots, at a silver car. On the hood of that car is Derek Palewski.

"No, that's a hybrid. That's Pam's car."

Derek's stretched out with a cigarette lighter in his hand, and he's reaching out to light Amy's cigarette. You're not technically supposed to smoke on school property, but somehow spandexers always get away with it—maybe because teachers don't want to come out here and bust them because it's too cold.

Derek says something, and a couple of senior spandexers wearing puffy winter coats with big fur-trimmed hoods laugh as if he said something hilarious.

"This looks like a scene from the Inuit version of *Grease*," I say.

"Ew, look at them," Aviva says, her voice muffled by her scarf and her collar. "They're worshipping him like a skeevy god."

"A skeevy god in a *T-shirt*," I add, taking a sip of Aviva's coffee before handing it back to her. "What is he doing?"

When we walk by, he's explaining his lack of a coat to the spandexers, who are bouncing up and down to keep the feeling in their legs and dragging on cigarettes.

"I'm *impervious*," Derek declares, raising his cigarette lighter. "I'm *impervious* to pain, and I'm *impervious* to cold. Here—feel my arm. No goose bumps!"

He holds out his arm, and the girls actually touch it, like it's a dinosaur bone during show-and-tell.

"What's your secret? How do you stay so warm?" one spandexer asks in awe.

"Here is a wilderness survival tip," Derek says very seriously. "The best way to share body heat is to get naked."

"Oh, yeah?" Pam, surrounded by a cloud of clove cigarette smoke, looks skeptical.

"Swear to God!" Derek says. "Skin-to-skin. Naked-to-naked. It's like electricity. You gotta *connect* to transfer the heat. And me? I got a lotta body heat.

"Who wants some?" he asks.

"That makes me so mad," Aviva says, holding her coffee away from her body as we jog the last few steps to the doors of the school. "No one whistles at me in the hallways anymore, and all these gross boys are getting attention they don't deserve."

The heat vents right inside the main hallway doors feel amazing. As we head to homeroom, Aviva continues her rant.

"Look at that! Robbie Hartmann is getting tongue!"

Kristin Chung is pressing Robbie Hartmann against the first locker in the south hallway and making out with him. Robbie Hartmann isn't completely gross, but his personality is about as exciting as clear nail polish.

"And Pirate Dave is getting free coffee!" Aviva fumes. "He's a pirate!" she calls out to two girls, who are delivering a hot drink and a scone to Dave at his locker.

Dave takes one sip from the paper cup and then gives it back, saying disdainfully, "I said *soy* milk."

"Spandexers always look for boyfriends when it gets cold out," I remind Aviva. "These girls want warm bodies to get them through winter."

"It's ridiculous!" Aviva says. "They're turning these slimeballs into kings."

Believe it or not, Aviva isn't the angriest person in the south hallway this morning. As we pass the senior lounge, Pam comes storming down the hallway. Inside the lounge, a group of girls surround Josh and Chung, who are sitting in the only two big comfy chairs. If Pirate Dave has groupies, you can imagine how well Josh and Chung are doing—they were both cute and popular before the boy recession.

"What's up, Pammy?" Josh asks as Pam storms in.

Pam drops a stack of papers and a pen in front of Josh.

"What's this?" he asks.

"A prom contract," Pam says.

Josh takes his feet off the table and glances at Chung, who's playing a game on his cell phone and only looks up to give his standard clueless shrug.

"In August, we agreed to go to the prom together this year," Pam reminds Josh. "So I'm just formalizing the agreement. You sign here"—she points to the first page—"and initial here."

"Shit," Josh says, shaking his head. "This thing is four pages? What does it say?"

"The first page is the agreement to be each other's dates," Pam says. "The second page says you'll pose with me for at least twenty-five pictures. The third page lists acceptable colors and styles for your tux. Read that carefully, because if you show up wearing a ruffled shirt, I am legally entitled to kick you in the crotch."

Josh is starting to sweat. He flips frantically through the contract. "Where was that part about my crotch? And what kind of shirt? What? I don't even remember talking to you about prom."

Pam pulls her agenda out of her bag and opens to a dog-eared page.

"August twenty-fourth, after two SoCo Lime shots at Amy's house party, you and I agreed to go to the prom together. Your verbal agreement constituted an oral contract."

"Wait, what?" says Chung, who's suddenly paying attention. He snaps his phone shut and grabs the contract from Josh. "There's oral stuff in here?"

Chung looks through the contract for about three minutes but doesn't find anything interesting, so he puts it down, saying, "No oral stuff."

"Maybe there should be," Josh says slyly, looking sideways at Pam. "Is there any, uh...hanky-panky clause in here?"

"Hanky-panky clause?" Pam asks in disgust. "You've got to be kidding me."

"I have options, ya know," Josh says. "I'm a hot commodity. A lot of girls would take me to prom, even with a ruffled shirt on."

Pam looms over Josh and starts to raise her voice.

"This is my senior prom. I've been on a diet for nine years, I already bought my dress, and I am not going alone. Now, you are a gigantic idiot, but you are a gigantic idiot who looks good in pictures, so sign this prom contract! Sign it!"

Josh ducks his head while he signs the first page and initials the rest. Chung waits until Pam is a safe distance away, and then snickers. "Sucker."

"I usually hate Pam and her vegan bitchery," Aviva

tells me as we stop at her locker so she can take off some of her layers. "But at least someone's laying down the law around here."

Just then, I see Hunter. He's leaning against a doorway across the hall from us, and there are three girls with him, one of whom is touching his hair.

"Do you use conditioner?" she asks.

"Nah," Hunter says. "I just rub a bar of soap on my head."

The girls crack up laughing. At first Hunter looks confused, but then he smiles. Next to me, Aviva starts to say something, but then she sees Hunter.

"He's not a slimeball," Aviva reassures me.

He's not a slimeball, I think, as we walk into our classroom, *but he is a king.*

CHAPTER 17: KELLY

"A World Without Men:
Singletons, Sperm Banks, and the
Soon-Approaching Man Apocalypse"

"The Boy Recession©" by Aviva Roth,
The Julius Journal, December

Kelly, do you have SAD?" Darcy asks me from across our cafeteria lunch table.

"What? Why?" I ask, looking up from the pasta that I'm pushing around with a plastic fork.

"You seem kind of...blah," Darcy says. "And your lunch is ninety-eight percent carbs."

SAD is seasonal affective disorder, a mild depression you can get in the winter if you don't get enough sunlight. We read about SAD last year in one of Aviva's *Glamour* articles—actually, we read about the "SAD diet," which is supposed to help you fight the urge to eat carbs all day.

"I'm going to get that light box back," Darcy tells me, jotting a note to herself in the presidential-seal notebook she always carries around. "I'm going to lobby with the administration."

Last year Julius had this huge fake-sun lamp in one of the exam rooms of the nurse's office. The school imported it from Sweden or Norway or whatever scarily northern country Björk comes from. They set it up in December and posted this sign-up sheet on the door so we could sign up for fifteen-minute slots of time with the light. That's how pathetic life is in Whitefish Bay—you have to sign up for a fifteen-minute time slot of fake sunlight. But this year is even more pathetic—we can't even afford fake sunlight. I guess it was part of the budget cuts.

"Okay, I'll use you as my case study," Darcy tells me. "Tell me about your symptoms. And how does it start? What triggers your depression?"

It's our last week of school before winter break, which is also the darkest week of the year, so I guess technically my mood could be caused by SAD. But I'm pretty sure that events that took place this morning actually triggered my depression.

I was in PMS, and Hunter called me over to use me as an example for his drum lesson. Hunter was showing our kids how to use brushes, instead of sticks, to play the drums. Hunter had me stand in front of his students, and he played my head with the brushes. They actually felt kind of nice in my hair, but they tickled, too. So I was laughing and looking up at Hunter, and all of the kids were laughing, and even Johann was smiling as he watched, when Diva burst in through the door that connects the band room with the stage.

"Hunter," she announced. "We have rehearsal right now."

"What?" Hunter stopped playing on my hair and handed the brushes down to one of his kids. "I'm teaching right now."

"Well, according to your schedule in the guidance office, you have a study hall now," Diva said. "Mrs. Martin looked it up."

I hated her so much. I hated her bossy voice and her too-tight pants and how you can always see the outline of her thong. The point of a thong is so people *can't* see your underwear, right?

"I don't have a study hall anymore. I just didn't have time to change my schedule because I'm busy," Hunter said. "And I'm busy right now, too."

I think that was the first time I ever heard Hunter sound pissed off. Actually, he didn't sound pissed off. He sounded...strict. He even turned his back to Diva and bent down to help his girl student use the brushes on her drum pad.

But Diva didn't leave. She came over to us and tried to put on her nice voice.

"We really need you, Hunter," Diva said. "Mrs. Martin wants to do our song. Plus, George is off-key on 'Mr. Cellophane.' He needs your help."

Hunter looked up, but not at Diva—at me. He sighed and gave me an apologetic look.

"I'm sorry," he said. "I just...They need me."

I was thinking *I need you, too,* so hard that I couldn't open my mouth or I would have said it out loud. But Johann spoke up before I could.

"I can take over the drums," he said.

Hunter walked out with Diva but turned around and said, "I'll be back—like, twenty minutes, tops."

He never came back. After we put the kids on the bus, I went backstage, where Diva and Hunter were rehearsing. As I saw them together, I was thinking one thing on repeat: *I'm losing him. I'm losing him. I'm losing him.*

But now, as Aviva comes to the table with her lunch— a large Diet Coke and three chocolate-chip cookies, which is not one of the meals recommended by the SAD diet—I try to push Hunter out of my mind.

"What's going on?" Aviva asks us.

"Kelly has seasonal depression," Darcy says.

"Well, I know what will cheer you up," Aviva tells me. "Let's have a girls' night out!"

As soon as she says it, Darcy and I groan.

"Girls' night out?" Darcy says. "Every night we go out is a girls' night out."

It's true. We spend most of our Friday and Saturday nights at Aviva's house, at the movies, or at Starbucks. Somehow we got the idea that Starbucks was the place to meet cute boys with glasses who would take us to concerts of bands we'd never heard of. But every time we go there, it's all crazy bearded men with newspapers and middle-aged divorcées on Match.com dates.

"Okay," Aviva sighs, breaking off a piece of her cookie and handing it to me. "It's actually for my column. I'm writing a column about girls' nights out."

Aviva's column, "The Boy Recession," has been a big success. Actually, it's titled "The Boy Recession" with a copyright symbol after it, because Eugene threatened to sue her. Her article "Skankology," documenting the increase in skanky behavior at our school, was really popular. She also wrote a great article about Pam's prom contract. Occasionally she covers some pretty serious stuff, like skewed gender ratios in China and the Middle East, or boy recessions on college campuses, but mostly she writes about Julius, and her articles get Tweeted and linked on Facebook all over the place.

"No way," Darcy says, shutting her notebook. "Please don't publish our pathetic lives so people can spread them all over the Internet. No one wants to read about us getting picked up from the movies by Kelly's dad in the station wagon. No offense, Kell."

"No, I completely agree."

"Well, then, give me some gossip to write about!" Aviva says.

"Wow," I say. "Look at Bobbi."

A few weeks back, Eugene unexpectedly broke up with Bobbi. His actions made a lot of girls really mad, and it proved that Eugene was the King of the Slimeball Kings. Everyone's been talking a lot of crap about him, except Bobbi, who would have a right to trash Eugene, who hasn't said one word against him. She keeps crying in the bathroom, but afterward she bravely reapplies her fake lashes and mascara before facing the world of Julius again.

Of course, you can still sense she isn't her usual carbonated self.

"Hi, girls," Bobbi says as she walks over to our table. "Hey, Darcy. I wrote up a report for the Healthy Lunch Initiative. I talked to Pam about sourcing some local organic products and projected some costs. I hope it's helpful."

When Darcy takes the report, she stares at it like she's amazed it wasn't written in pink glitter glue.

"So how are you girls doing?" Bobbi asks Aviva and me, sitting down at our table.

"We're okay," I say cautiously. "How are *you*, Bobbi?"

Bobbi's eyes fill with tears, and I'm frightened for her makeup. Apparently Aviva is, too, because she panics and bursts out: "We're planning a girls' night out!"

Bobbi's face lights up. The eye makeup is saved.

"That sounds like so much fun!" Bobbi says. "We should *totally* do that!"

Darcy tears herself away from the Excel chart long enough to shoot Aviva a death stare.

"We're actually really boring," Darcy tells Bobbi. "We just go to Starbucks every weekend."

"I love Starbucks!" Bobbi chirps, meeting Darcy's eyes in wonder, like it's an unbelievably miraculous coincidence that four teenage girls would all like overpriced coffee with whipped cream on top.

"We should all go sometime," I say, trying to be tactful. "Maybe after winter break? Or after midterms?"

"What about this Friday?" Bobbi suggests. "Are you girls doing anything then?"

I look at Darcy, Darcy looks at Aviva, and Aviva shrugs and says honestly, "No. We're not doing anything."

"Look at this place," Aviva says in disbelief, as the Starbucks door chimes closed behind us on Friday night.

"*Aww!*" Bobbi says, coming in behind Darcy and stomping the snow off her boots. "It's all Christmassy in here!"

But Aviva isn't talking about the Christmas decorations; she's talking about the boys. Right when we walk in, there's a whole table of college guys in baseball caps and fleeces holding Venti-size drinks. There's a nerdy cute guy at the corner table, working on his laptop with his headphones on, and two preppy guys are working on a school project by the window.

When we go up to order our drinks, even the guys behind the counter are cute. The one making the drinks, who has a lip ring, gives Bobbi a free extra shot in her caramel latte.

"Okay, I'm kidnapping her and making her my AP physics experiment," Darcy tells me, dunking her green-tea bag like she's trying to drown a sixteenth-century witch. We're waiting for my Frappuccino while Aviva and Bobbi snag a table.

"I mean, this is incredible. All the variables are the same. This is the same Starbucks we always come to. This is the same time we're always here. The only thing that's different is that we brought Bobbi. Does she literally *attract* boys?"

It looks like it. By the time Darcy and I bring our drinks to the table, one of the college guys has already approached Bobbi, asking her if he should get a latte or a macchiato. Then the nerdy cute guy takes off his headphones to ask Bobbi if she can unplug his computer for him. He obviously wants to try to talk to her but is too shy. Bobbi just unplugs the computer with a smile, says, "Here you go," and turns back to us.

"Hey, Bobbi," Aviva says as she lounges in a big, comfy armchair. "That guy in the hat was kinda cute. I think you two would look good together."

Uh-oh. Here comes sad Barbie face again. I reach out and touch Bobbi's arm.

"Aw! What's wrong?" I ask.

"I can't even look at another guy," Bobbi says, dabbing at her eyeliner with her fake nail. "I'm still so in love with Eugene."

"*Really?*" Darcy asks. I kick her under the table.

"What actually happened between you and Eugene?" Aviva asks.

"I have no idea!" Bobbi says. "Everything was going great! We had *so* much fun together."

"Did you fight a lot?" Aviva asks, in her sensitive Oprah voice, nodding encouragingly to prove she's listening.

"Never!" Bobbi shakes her head.

"Did you sense him pulling away?"

"Not at all," Bobbi says. "Eugene was the *best* boyfriend. He came to all my tennis games, brought me Dunkachinos to my fourth-period study hall, and learned how to make sushi because he knows how much I love California rolls. He took my dad golfing and gave him stock tips. He called me every night before I went to sleep to tell me he loved me...."

Really? Pervy Eugene did all this? Darcy and I raise our eyebrows at each other.

"But, Bobbi," Darcy says, "don't you think it's for the best? Honestly, no one thought Eugene was good enough for you. I mean, look at the guys you've dated before. Justin Messina was smart and tall and really hot. Plus, he didn't have to clean out his locker before the cops brought the drug-sniffing dog around school."

Aviva and I aren't sure how Bobbi will take this, so we pretend to be very interested in our drinks. But Bobbi isn't offended.

"Those things don't matter to me," she says. "I've

dated tall guys and good-looking guys and college athletes and male models and..."

"Obviously the boy recession hits some of us harder than others," I tell Aviva behind my cup as Bobbi goes on with her list.

"But there's nothing," Bobbi tells Darcy, "like a boyfriend who really loves you for who you are."

This is exactly the kind of cheesy sentiment Darcy hates, like that quote girls have on their Facebook pages about special girls who "don't get picked" because they're "like apples at the top of a tree" or some crap like that. So when Bobbi goes to get the cinnamon shaker, I wait for the patented Darcy Ryan eye roll. But it doesn't happen. Darcy is just sitting there, holding her tea and looking thoughtful.

When Bobbi comes back, she seems a little happier. Maybe it was that cinnamon.

"I do love Eugene," she tells us. "But I guess if he doesn't want to be in a relationship, I should forget about him for now. Maybe it would actually be good to talk to another guy and get my mind off him. Do you think I should spill my drink on my iPhone and ask the guy with the headphones to reprogram it for me?"

"Definitely," Aviva says. "If nothing else, another guy will make Eugene jealous."

As Aviva helps Bobbi destroy her very expensive phone in the name of new love, I think about Hunter and Diva. If

Hunter is forgetting about me, then I should forget about him. The only problem with that is, unlike Bobbi, I don't have a coffeehouse full of willing guys at my disposal. *It took me long enough to find one guy I like. Where am I going to find another one?*

CHAPTER 18: HUNTER

"Slimeball Kings:
How Julius Slackers Rose to the Top of the Heap"

"The Boy Recession©" by Aviva Roth,
The Julius Journal, January

When I wake up on New Year's Day, I have the worst headache ever, and I'm in a purple sleeping bag. I don't remember whose sleeping bag it is, but it's definitely not mine.

It takes me an excruciating second to remember I'm at the *Chicago* cast sleepover at this sophomore girl Kerry's house. Last night all thirty of us were hanging out together, but now all the sleeping bags around me are empty. There's a rolled-up Twister mat and a bunch of plastic wineglasses scattered around the room, but no people. I guess everyone is upstairs.

I'd never heard of a coed sleepover before, and I'm pretty sure most people's parents wouldn't be too happy about it, but I told my parents I was sleeping at Eugene's, so they didn't know, and Kerry's parents don't know anything because they're away at their cabin for the weekend. I guess this sleepover thing is a tradition, and this year, I got invited.

Actually, I've been invited to a lot of stuff lately. It started when Bobbi would invite Eugene places, and Eugene would bring me and the D-Bags along. Bobbi always knew someone who was having people over to drink or watch a movie or go in somebody's hot tub. Before Eugene asked Bobbi out, I had no clue anyone in Whitefish Bay had a hot tub.

And once rehearsals for *Chicago* got going, the chorus girls from the show started inviting me places, too. I get the girls in the chorus mixed up—maybe because a lot of them have K names: Kerry, Kaitlyn, Kara. In the show, we do this big dance number called "All I Care About Is Love," during which all the girls sing "We want Billy. . . . We need Billy. . . ." before I burst through the doors and onto the stage.

That song kind of explains my life right now. I mean, people aren't singing songs about me in the school hallways, but last night, when I walked into the sleepover with Eugene and a case of champagne, the girls went berserk.

Squinting my eyes and looking around the room, I spot Eugene stretched out on a really nice couch. Eugene *would* get a couch all to himself and leave me stranded on the floor in some random sleeping bag. Too bad I'm not allowed to bitch at Eugene today.

"Hey, gingerbread boy," I say, but my voice is so shot that it barely registers.

So I throw a pillow at Eugene's head.

"What's up?" he croaks.

"Happy birthday," I tell him, unzipping the purple sleeping bag to get my legs free.

"Happy New Year," Eugene tells me, sitting up and right away feeling between the couch cushions for his BlackBerry.

"I feel like shit," I tell him. "My head hurts so bad."

"It's the sugary drinks," Eugene says. "They give you the worst hangovers. Your body can't metabolize sugar and alcohol at the same time. You're probably dehydrated."

I would kill for a Pepsi right now. A huge glass of really fizzy Pepsi with lots of ice cubes.

"Oh, man, what a night," Eugene says, tossing his BlackBerry to the other side of the couch and stretching his arms over his head.

Eugene's not in *Chicago*, but I brought him to the sleepover anyway, because it's his birthday and he didn't have any plans. He broke up with Bobbi about two weeks ago. I think their problems started when she showed him her promise ring. At first, Eugene thought she was only wearing it to be like all those girls on the Disney Channel, but it turned out Bobbi is actually pretty religious. She's so into the whole purity thing she wouldn't even let him touch her boobs. After a while it drove him crazy, being around that amazing rack and not being able to do anything about it. Then he started spending time with all these freshman girls and the temptation got to him. Yeah, I know—he's a horny, douchey bastard. I agree. Apparently he gave Bobbi a big breakup speech that was a big load of bullshit, about how he was like the Tin Man from *The Wizard of Oz* and she was the Wizard, who gave him a heart, but their journey on the Yellow Brick Road had come to an end, and blah, blah, blah. Eugene said Bobbi burst out crying.

But now Eugene is free to flirt with any chorus girl who's dumb enough to humor him. And he did plenty of flirting last night. He was loving all the drunken chorus girls. Kerry made us play all these games — Twister, Catch Phrase, charades — but the chorus girls turned them into drinking games. Lemme tell you, these girls can drink.

"We've got mimosas!" Kerry announces loudly, coming down the basement stairs holding a tray of drinks.

Oh, crap. Here we go again.

Eugene takes one off the tray, but I don't. Even the thought of alcohol makes my stomach hurt. Then I see Diva come downstairs, and my stomach hurts for a whole different reason. I suddenly remember who owns the purple sleeping bag and why I was in it. *Oh, crap, oh, crap, oh, crap.*

Last night at midnight we did the whole New Year's countdown thing, and everyone started grabbing one another and making out. Kerry was kissing George, Eugene was doing some creepy three-way kiss with two sophomore chorus girls, and Diva jumped on me. She'd been trying to hang out with me all night, saying we should be on teams together for charades and Catch Phrase, because we're both leads in the play and whatever. Then after midnight we made out on the couch for a while, until Eugene kicked us off so that he could go to sleep. I didn't have anywhere to sleep, so Diva made me share her purple sleeping bag. When I see Diva, I get the urge to jet out of the room as fast as possible. But apparently she doesn't feel the same way, because she comes right over to the couch and sits next to me and kind of snuggles.

"How'd you sleep?" she asks me, reaching up to touch my hair.

"Uh...okay," I say, avoiding her eyes.

"I told you my sleeping bag was really comfy!" Diva says. "It was comfy, right?"

"Uh-huh."

"You didn't get a mimosa?" she asks. "I'll get you one."

"No, I'm good," I say quickly. "I'm in more of a Pepsi place right now."

"I'll get you a Pepsi!" Diva says, popping up from the couch.

Man, I gotta get out of here. I try to give Eugene the escape signal, but he's too busy flirting. He's asking Kerry and her friends about their New Year's resolutions, and they're telling him about how they want to go to the gym and try that exercise class where you use a stripper pole, and Eugene's telling them that he knows a guy who could install stripper poles for them in their rooms.

"You know what *your* New Year's resolution should

be?" Kerry says to Eugene, putting down her tray of mimosas. "You should be in the musical next year!"

"Yeah! Yeah!" All the girls are agreeing. "Eugene, you *have* to be in the musical next year!"

Diva comes downstairs holding my dream Pepsi—the glass is huge and filled with ice cubes. It's ridiculously fizzy, too. After a few sips, my mouth doesn't feel so dry anymore, and the throbbing in my head chills out a little bit. And I realize I'm actually pretty hungry.

"I think me and Eugene are gonna go," I tell Diva, getting up off the couch, where she was smashed up against me.

"You should stay!" Diva says. "We're making bacon and eggs upstairs."

Man, bacon and eggs sounds good. Maybe this girl isn't so bad—purple sleeping bag, Pepsi, bacon. . . . But if I don't tear Eugene away from these chorus girls, we're gonna be here forever. So I tell him I've got a birthday surprise waiting for him and drag him away.

Diva calls out to me, "I'll text you later," which throws me off, because I had no clue she had my phone number. *When did that happen?* But I just say, "Cool," and head out the door.

I don't actually have a birthday surprise for Eugene, but I have my wallet, so I take him to IHOP for breakfast. Eugene gets steak tips and eggs, and I get a Smokehouse Combo with sausage links and hash browns and extra bacon. When I look up from my food, I notice that Eugene's on his BlackBerry.

"Hey," I say, spitting out little bits of sausage. "Stop texting."

"I'm on Facebook," he says. "I love being on Facebook on my birthday. Everyone's sending me messages and writing on my wall. *And* I already got a bunch of friend requests from your chorus girls. And pokes."

"Very nice."

"Do you think Kerry and Katie would ever be interested in a kind of... PG-thirteen threesome?"

"Weird," I say. "Which Katie?"

"Katie R."

"No way in hell. Don't even try it."

"Hey, look at this," Eugene says.

"What?"

"Is this true?"

"What?"

"Diva Price is in a relationship," Eugene says.

"What? She has a boyfriend?"

Crap. Crap. Is some steroid-chugging douche from Milwaukee gonna come beat me up because his girlfriend forced me into her purple sleeping bag? And if Diva has a boyfriend, why was she groping me on New Year's Eve?

"Doesn't say," Eugene says. "It just says *in a relationship.* And... Oh, this is interesting."

"What?"

"She just changed her relationship status to 'in a relationship,' like, ten minutes ago."

"Huh? What does that mean?"

Eugene puts his BlackBerry down on his napkin and looks at me intensely across all our breakfast meats.

"Huntro," he says. "Tell me what happened last night."

"I dunno! She just, like, jumped me. We hooked up on the couch for a while, and then we were in that sleeping bag....I don't know! I guess at some point she got my phone number, but I don't remember that."

"Is it possible at some point you asked her out and you don't remember that?" Eugene asks.

"Nah. No way."

"Or *she* asked *you* out and you don't remember?"

"Nah..." I hesitate. "I don't think so. No, right?"

"I don't know, Huntro."

I stop eating mid-sausage.

"What do I do?" I ask Eugene.

"Well, why not go with it?" Eugene says. "I mean, I like being single, but this doesn't seem like a girl who's gonna pull a promise ring on you."

"Yeah. I guess not."

I guess Diva's not that bad. At times she's attractive, and she does seem to like me.

"And this could be your only chance to get a girlfriend. Not that you're not adorable, Huntro. But you never ask anyone out. I mean, do you have anything else going on?"

Kelly Robbins pops into my head. But Kelly is really pretty and cool and totally chill. And who the hell am I? A sweaty bacon-eating guy who spent the night drunk in a weird sleeping bag.

"I guess not," I say.

"This girl fell in your lap," Eugene says. "Lemme tell ya, it doesn't get much easier than that."

"Yeah," I say.

I lean back against the booth and stretch my arms above my head. I guess I'll just deal with this when I have to. I mean, she didn't ask me to change my relationship status.

CHAPTER 19: KELLY

"Flirting via Facebook:
Be a Vixen without Catching a Virus"

"The Boy Recession©" by Aviva Roth,
The Julius Journal, January

Being in Darcy's room is like being called into the principal's office. All the shelves above her huge desk are full of binders and not-fun books such as *America's Top Universities* and *SAT vs. ACT: The Most Important Choice of Your Life*.

"Explain the 'gospel of wealth' that was embraced during the Gilded Age," Darcy demands, spinning around on her imposing desk chair.

Aviva is sitting cross-legged on the end of Darcy's bed, flipping through our textbook, looking for attractive men from American history for her special midterm column on historical hotties. According to her, they started getting attractive only after 1805.

"I think I like the Gilded Age," she observes. "Amazing houses, rich guys with big mustaches . . . Maybe I should help to bring the bushy mustache back in style!"

"You think you have that kind of influence?" I ask. "You can bring back the bushy mustache?"

"I'm a trendsetter in the blogosphere," Aviva informs me. "One hundred sixty-three people like my blog on Facebook. Some of them are random Canadians."

"How did random Canadians find your blog?" I ask.

"Excuse me," Darcy interrupts our conversation. "Are we here to study or what?"

Every year, we have a two-and-a-half-week winter break at Julius: The first week and a half is holiday vacation, and the next week you're supposed to spend studying for midterms. Of course, it's another one of Julius's terrible ideas; people like Aviva consider it an extra-long vacation, and people like Darcy consider it no vacation at all, because she'll study the whole time. I try to have one week of fun and one week of studying. But this year I made a mistake: I went on Facebook. I swear I was only gonna go on for five minutes, check a few photo albums, get my distraction impulses out of the way, and then buckle down with studying. And then I saw Diva Price's relationship status. She had one of those red hearts next to her name— suddenly I hated Mark Zuckerberg for inventing those red hearts—and it said "Diva Price is in a relationship."

I hoped she wasn't in a relationship with Hunter. Then the status updates started popping up.

Three months until Chicago, starring @Hunter Fahrenbach and...ME!

Should be studying, but someone keeps texting me...@Hunter Fahrenbach!

Can't wait to get back to rehearsals with my boo!

And that's when I made a resolution to move on and find a new guy—at least while Hunter is with Diva. I'm going to stop liking him and stop thinking about him. I mean, Bobbi got two phone numbers at Starbucks that night before winter break. If Bobbi can move on from Eugene, then I can move on from Hunter. The only problem with moving on is that everywhere I go has Wi-Fi access, and I can't stop myself from logging on to Diva's Facebook page to see her latest gross, annoying status. It seems like there's only one place I'm safe: Darcy's house. She shuts off her wireless router for all of study week, to reduce distractions.

I slide off the bed to check out the snack situation on Darcy's desk. It's depressing: dried fruit, pretzels, and nuts. I'm sick of healthy food, and I'm sick of studying.

"Can't we take a break?" I ask Darcy. "We've been studying for, like, two hours. We need to find me a new crush."

"Ooh, the Astors were good-looking." Aviva is dog-earing a page of her textbook. "Do you think they've got some great-great-grandsons kickin' around? An Astor could be good for you, Kell."

"One of them went down on the *Titanic*, remember?" Darcy says. "Viva, you watch that movie every weekend."

"*Ooh*, right! J.J.! He had that pregnant wife. Did she get in a lifeboat? I can't remember. *Ooh*, let's watch *Titanic* tonight."

"No, we're supposed to be finding me a new boy to like," I remind her.

"We're supposed to be studying U.S. history!" Darcy reminds both of us.

"We're taking a break from that," I tell her. "Darcy, you're a good brainstormer. Where can I meet a new guy to like, considering I don't have a car or a fake ID and our whole town is snowed in?"

Darcy surrenders and comes over to the bed, bringing her lame snacks with her. Pretty soon all the almonds are gone, and half of the dried cherries, and we still haven't thought of a new guy for me. "Okay, I have a better book," Aviva says, getting up to grab something from Darcy's desk. When she comes back with it, she moves a pillow so she can snuggle between us.

"What is this?" I take the white booklet out of her hand.

"The snow-day phone chain!"

"Oh, that's romantic," Darcy says.

"Well, it has the phone number of every guy at Julius," Aviva says, and opens it up to start looking. The listings are separated by class, so Aviva flips to the back to start with the seniors. But there are so few available seniors left, and juniors, that she ends up at the sophomores in less than a minute.

"What do you think about going younger?" Aviva asks, wiggling her eyebrows. "That whole cougar thing?"

"The cougar trend happened, like, two years ago," Darcy says.

"But all trendy stuff takes a while to get to Wisconsin," Aviva says. "What about really young? *Oooh*, let's check out the freshmen."

Aviva flips to the front of the book, and I see a familiar name.

"I guess I could..." I begin, but then I stop myself.

"What?" Aviva prompts me. "Who? Which one?"

"Well, I know him...." I point to the page. "Johann."

"Johann? *Ooh*, he sounds exotic," Aviva says. "Is that German?"

"The piccolo kid?" Darcy asks. "From PMS?"

"Common interests!" Aviva claps. "You both like music!"

"Do you know anything else about him?" Darcy asks. "Is he smart? Is he nice? Who is he friends with?"

I pick some dried cherries off the tray and count them into my palm.

"I think he's smart. He knows a lot about music. His dad's a music professor, he said. He's kind of shy. I don't know if he has too many friends. He is nice, though."

"*Hmmm...*" Aviva muses, reaching over to pick a dried cherry out of my hand. "This could really work."

"What do you mean?"

"Well, in PMS, it's only you and him and Hunter,

right? So Hunter will be able to witness your budding romance firsthand."

"Budding?" Darcy raises an eyebrow.

"Nothing makes a guy realize he likes you more than seeing you with another guy," Aviva continues. "And if you date this Johann guy, Hunter will see you with him, for two hours, every week."

So after much prodding from Aviva, I pick up Darcy's desk phone and dial Johann's number.

"Hello?"

This is definitely not Johann. "Hi, um, can I speak with Johann, please?"

"Who is speaking, if I may ask?"

"It's, um, Kelly. Robbins."

"Please hold on one moment," the voice tells me.

When he puts down the phone, I spin my chair around and mouth to Darcy and Aviva, *Johann's dad sounds like Arnold Schwarzenegger.* Both of them giggle, so I start giggling, but I have to stop once Johann picks up the phone and says in his quiet, polite voice, "Hello?"

"Hi, Johann? It's Kelly."

"I know. . . . Uh, my dad told me. How are you?"

For some reason, I feel this sudden need to confess to him.

"I got your number off the snow-day phone chain!" I burst out.

"Oh . . ." Johann says uncertainly. "Is school canceled tomorrow?"

"No!" I say. "Actually, yes, it is canceled, because it's study week. But I…"

"Oh, right." Johann laughs a little, nervously. "Study week."

"But I… That's not why I called."

I spin back around to get some support, and Darcy and Aviva look up from a picture of a young Franklin Roosevelt to give me a thumbs-up.

"I wanted to know if you wanted to go out sometime…."

"More specific!" Darcy hisses from behind me.

"… or Friday," I continue. "Because I wanted to talk to you about teaching music! And…music. And stuff."

What a lame ending. And how many times did I just say "wanted"? *Ugh. I am so awkward.*

"Oh, to talk about teaching? Is Hunter coming?" Johann says.

"No. Just you and me," I say. "I wanted to…get to know you. So Friday is good? What about Kopp's, to get custard? Eight o'clock?"

"Okay…That sounds good," Johann says, polite but cautious.

"Okay, good! So I'll meet you there!"

I'm so anxious to get off the phone and be done with this whole thing that I almost end the call before Johann speaks up.

"Um…Kelly? Can you…Do you think you could pick me up? Because…uh…I can't drive, so —"

"Right! Sure! Yeah, I'll…I'll pick you up at eight."

CHAPTER 20: HUNTER

"Caveman to Cutie:
What Bio Class Can Teach Us About
the Evolution of the Male Mind"

"The Boy Recession©" by Aviva Roth,
The Julius Journal, January

I think this place is, like, withering my soul away," I tell Eugene in the fourth aisle of Office Depot, one of Eugene's favorite places. He comes here all the time to buy supplies for his business, so he knows what's in every aisle. But today we're shopping for me. I, Hunter Fahrenbach, am buying an agenda.

Eugene ignores the comment about my withering soul.

"This is a beautiful model," he says, holding up this fancy-looking day planner. "Full-zip nylon cover, titanium clasp...Ooh, recycled paper! Gotta go green, Hunter. Gotta go green."

I take the planner and flip through the pages. There's already stuff written on a bunch of days. Christmas, Hanukkah, daylight saving time, Canadian Thanksgiving... *Ugh.*

I can't handle all these commitments. I put the planner back on the shelf and run my hand through my hair. On Saturday, I got my first real haircut since sixth grade. It's for the musical. Mrs. Martin, Pam, and Amy decided Billy Flynn can't have hair that touches his shoulders, and they didn't go for my ponytail idea, either. So it was a haircut against my will. It's really, really short.

"Stop messing with it," Eugene tells me. "It's supposed to have that part in it. You can't mess with the part."

"I hate having my hair parted," I tell him. "It's too neat. I look like one of the Hitler Youth. This is a politically incorrect haircut."

I rub my hand all over my head to mess up my hair.

"Stop!" Eugene says. "It looks good! It definitely looks better than before. You look professional. I'd consider hiring you with that haircut."

"No, thanks," I tell him, shoving my hands into the pockets of my winter coat. "I already have too much shit to do."

"So what are you looking for?" Eugene says, turning back to shelves full of agendas. "A weekly? A daily?"

"I guess I need a daily. People are giving me homework every day, and since I effed up my midterms, I actually have to do some of it. And I have rehearsal every night. Even Fridays."

Rehearsing on Friday nights sucks. All my online *World of Warcraft* buddies are missing my sword-wielding skills, and my actual three-dimensional friends are missing me, too. I have zero time to drive around with Derek, shooting at people's mailboxes with paintball guns.

Being in this musical is like living under a Fascist regime. You should see these rehearsals. Last night the choreographer, Amy, screamed at us so much she lost her voice.

"Box step! Box step!"

"Kick ball change! *No!* Kick ball change!"

"*One*-two-three-four! *One*-two-three-four!"

"Chorus girl in the back! Turn *left*! Do you not see everyone else turning to the *left*?"

"Billy Flynn! Bigger arms, Billy Flynn!"

"Shuffle step, Billy Flynn!"

I am so sick of hearing "Billy Flynn." Every time I hear that damn name, I cringe. While we're on the subject, I'm sick of my own name, too. In these books my dad reads about how to get a job, they say people love to hear their own names. Don't try it with me. I'm sick of hearing "Hunter" everywhere I go. In class, teachers are calling on me every five minutes; now that my hair is short, they can see my face, and they remember to call on me.

In pre-calc: "Hunter, how do you factor this quadratic?"

In U.S. history: "Hunter, how did FDR fight the Great Depression?"

In gym: "Hunter, you're a captain today. Pick your floor-hockey team."

In AP chem: "Hunter, where's your lab report?"

My lab report is still missing, actually.... Which is

where this planner comes in. But I have to look at them myself, because Eugene is screwing around over by the accordion folders.

"Twenty-four ninety-nine?" I balk, turning one over. "There's no way I'm dropping twenty-five bucks on this thing!"

But Eugene is down at the end of the aisle now, opening binders and flipping through them.

"Yo, gingerbread boy!" I call to him. "I need your help with this!"

"I've got my own stuff to buy," he tells me. Eugene holds up a big red binder and asks me, "Do you think this will hold head shots?"

"Head shots?" I groan. "Dude, please tell me you're not taking pictures of girls you're hooking up with."

Eugene has been sharing *waaaaay* too much about his hookups with me since he broke up with Bobbi.

"Nope," Eugene says. "This is for my new business project. I'm selling prom dates!"

"Huh?"

"Well, I'm sure you've noticed how the lovely women of our school are already worrying about the prom," Eugene says, reaching for a green binder on a high shelf. "I myself have already been asked three times."

Eugene is too short to reach the green binder, so I grab it for him.

"Isn't the prom in, like, June?"

"May," Eugene corrects me. "And the young women of

Julius P. Heil are way ahead of us in thinking about it. Women are planners, Huntro. It's one of the advantages they have over us. Look at Pam. This girl is already making money off the prom. She's hawking that overpriced prom contract of hers all over town."

"You always make money off the prom," I say. "You bought, like, five hundred dollars' worth of beer for the limos last year."

"Well, this year I'm selling alcohol *and* men."

"Selling men? Dude, isn't that a little...illegal?"

We head back to the planners as Eugene explains.

"Just think of me like a professional matchmaker," he says. "I'll provide a selection of clean, well-groomed, well-mannered young men to serve as escorts for the evening. Well, not *escorts*."

"Where are you gonna find these dudes?"

"I'm going into Milwaukee to recruit at a bunch of private schools. Then I'm gonna hit up some sports events for the jock types, concerts for my emo guys, support groups for those sensitive new-age men."

"Very nice."

"And perhaps the rock-star type as well?" Eugene says, pressing an agenda into my chest and looking at me questioningly.

"What?" I don't even take the agenda. "What, you want me? To be a prostitute?"

"To be a *prescreened escort*," Eugene corrects me. "You could earn two hundred dollars! Girls like you now,

Huntro. You've got that guitar thing going on. And I wasn't totally committed to that *well-groomed* part of the deal."

"Yeah, well, thanks for the compliment," I say. "But I have a girlfriend, remember? Thanks to you pushing me into it, I have a girlfriend. And I'm pretty sure she would not be cool with me hiring myself out."

I'm also pretty sure that Diva is going to force me to take her to the prom. And I'm sure she'll force me to wear some ridiculous suit and buy her flowers and rent a limo. My so-called girlfriend is a psycho. Every free second I have, she's texting me about dumb stuff, like my clothes. On Sunday night, she let me know that I should wear "that green shirt" to school on Monday. I actually remembered, and wore it, but when she saw me in the morning, she was pissed off.

"I said the *green* shirt," she said.

I looked down and pulled the shirt away from my chest to see the color.

"This is green."

"It's *blue*."

So on top of all the other crap I'm dealing with, I think I'm color-blind.

"Hunter! I got a surprise for you!"

As soon as I walk in the door, my dad is all over me. He's holding a bunch of DVDs.

"Check these out: *Singin' in the Rain, West Side Story, Phantom of the Opera, Fiddler on the Roof.* I asked the guy at the counter for musicals with strong male leads. This Billy Flynn is a great character, but in *Chicago*, it's all about the girls. Next year they should do *Phantom*. You need a male lead with a dark side."

"Uh-huh," I say, sitting on the stairs and dropping the bag with my new agenda in it. When I first got cast as Billy Flynn, my dad rented *Chicago* the movie, and he got really into it.

"Whadda you think, movie marathon tonight?" my dad asks. "I got popcorn, too! None of that organic crap Mom gets. Real popcorn."

"Uh, maybe later," I tell my dad. "I gotta take a nap first."

I leave the agenda on the stairs and drag my ass into the kitchen. I just need five minutes to myself, during which I can make a grilled cheese with half a stick of butter.

"Hunter!" my dad calls. "You're not eating dairy, are you? I read it messes with your vocal cords!"

CHAPTER 21: KELLY

"Cougars Among Us:
Julius Juniors and Their Freshman Boy-Toys"

"The Boy Recession©" by Aviva Roth,
The Julius Journal, February

I don't know if it's from being shut inside for months or lowered immunity from my SAD, but for two weeks I've had this horrible cold that won't go away. I don't feel sick enough to go home, but I can't play the flute because I'm coughing so hard. On Tuesday, we were teaching the flutes their first notes, and after I interrupted our lesson for my fifth coughing attack, Johann suggested cautiously, "Why don't you go get a drink? I can take over here."

When Johann said that, Hunter looked over at us and smiled, which made me realize that he knows we're dating. Maybe he read Aviva's stupid article about Julius cougars, which didn't mention me by name but might has well have. Is there any other junior girl dating a "musically inclined freshman with a penchant for clogs and diminutive woodwind instruments"? I don't think so.

So Hunter knows, but he hasn't said anything. Last week it seemed like he was in a bad mood, and I hoped he was a little upset about me dating someone, but it turned out he was just tired from musical rehearsal.

Today, after our PMS lesson, I'm sitting on the piano bench, feeling sorry for myself. Hunter is on the bandstand, putting the drum set back together, and Johann comes over to me.

"How are you feeling?" he asks.

"I'm okay," I say, sighing. "But I don't think I can go to the movie tonight. I just don't want to cough through the whole thing."

"Okay, no problem at all," Johann says politely. "Oh, and, um, my mother gave me something for you. This tea. It's for colds, I guess. But if you don't want it, you..."

He takes an envelope out of his pocket and hands it to me.

"That's so sweet! Thank you so much. Thank her for me," I say, before I start coughing again.

"I can call you tonight, if you want," Johann offers.

"Sure! Yeah."

"Is eight o'clock okay?"

"Oh, you can call whenever. I'll be home all night, so..."

"Okay. I'll call at eight, if that's okay."

"Okay. Eight is perfect."

Johann kind of nods at me and walks away, and I sit on that piano bench, holding his mother's Austrian tea, counting how many times we just said "okay" to each other, and thinking, *So this is what it's like to have a boyfriend.* It's not exactly a Taylor Swift song.

Taylor Swift is always singing about front porches and screen doors, stars and lakes. In her songs, there's always a boy in a truck, or a boy throwing rocks at a window, and it's always a dewy summer night, and everyone's always kissing by a lake. In my life, there are no guys driving trucks or throwing rocks at windows. That's not Johann's fault, though. I mean, he just turned fifteen, so he can't drive. I guess if he wanted to throw rocks at my window, he'd have to walk or have his dad drive him. But that wouldn't be very spontaneous.

Not that Johann is spontaneous. He is definitely a planner. The couple of times that we've gone to the movies, we picked them three days in advance, and Johann read all the reviews. I picked him up in my dad's station wagon, and he paid for the tickets. The first time we went out, I tried to give him money, but he said, "I couldn't allow you to pay." In some ways, I'm really lucky. I doubt any other girl I know has a boyfriend who takes her out and holds the door for her and brings her Austrian tea. The way things are going around here, I may be the closest thing to Taylor Swift that Julius has right now. Of course, Taylor Swift usually kisses the boys in her songs, and Johann and I haven't kissed yet. But it's probably my fault. I've had this phlegmy cold almost the whole time we've been going out. Every time I talk to someone, I end up hacking in their face until they run away or politely hold a folder in front of their face. I don't know how long I've been sitting on the piano bench, spacing out, when Hunter knocks over the cymbals and they clatter against the bandstand.

"Sorry, sorry!" Hunter says, popping his head up from behind the drum set. "Did I freak you out?"

"No." I shake my head. "I think I'm in a NyQuil haze."

Hunter takes a big leap over a bass drum and comes down from the bandstand.

"Whoa," he says, looking down at me. "That tea smells pretty strong."

"Does it?" I hold the envelope up to my nose and sniff. "I can't even smell it, I'm so stuffed up."

I put the tea down and take a tissue out of my pocket to blow my nose. But Hunter stops me. As soon as I bring the tissue to my face, he reaches down and pinches the fattest part of my nose.

"Wait, stop," he says.

I look up at him over his hand and ask, "What are you doing?" But my voice is nasal from having my nose pinched, and that makes both of us laugh.

"You're not supposed to blow your nose," Hunter says.

"I'm not?"

"No one is. It's bad to blow your nose. Seriously! I read something about it. Blowing your nose makes your head explode or something."

I guess I'm making a horrified face as I look at him,

breathing through my mouth, because Hunter laughs and corrects himself.

"Not *explode,* I guess. But it's something about the pressure in your head."

I don't take the tissue away from my face, so Hunter doesn't take his fingers off my nose.

"I'm probably really snotty," I apologize.

"It's okay," he says, and leans down and whispers in my ear, "my hand isn't that clean, anyway."

I laugh, and Hunter lets me use my tissue.

"Hey, so you and Johann are going out?" he asks as I cross the room to the garbage can.

I'm glad that my back is turned when I say, "Yeah, I guess so."

"That's cool," Hunter says. "He's cool."

When I get back to the piano, I ask, "How'd you know? Did you read Aviva's article?"

"What?"

"In the school newspaper."

"Oh, no," Hunter, says, moving his legs so I can sit on the bench. "I just heard you talking about taking him to the movies. So I figured either he needed someone to get him into a PG-thirteen movie, or..."

He's making fun of me. I can't believe he's making fun of me. I look up at him with my mouth open.

"He's fifteen!"

"I know, I know," Hunter says, laughing.

"He's not that young!" I protest. "He'll be able to drive soon! Well, in, like, a year."

"No, but seriously," Hunter says, "he's a good guy! He is. He's smart, and he knows his stuff with music. And he's very...ironed."

Hunter runs his hand down the front of his own shirt, which is very...not ironed. Hunter's shirt is faded and wrinkled, and his knees are coming through the holes in his jeans.

"That's probably good for you, right? An...ironed... guy?" Hunter asks me, drumming absentmindedly on his bare knees with his fingers.

"I thought so," I say, trying not to sound too miserable, watching Hunter's hands the whole time.

CHAPTER 22: KELLY

"Promise Rings or Pretense? The Reality Behind Julius's Celibacy Trend"

"The Boy Recession©" by Aviva Roth,
The Julius Journal, February

We thought this was the perfect day to tell you how much you mean to us," a freshman girl says to Pirate Dave as she hands him a huge bouquet of expensive-looking flowers.

Dave takes the bouquet in one hand and examines it critically.

"Are these hybrid tea roses?" he asks.

"Well, the florist guy didn't say...." the girl says.

Dave sighs and slams his locker.

"To be honest, I prefer American beauties," he tells her. He gives back the bouquet and walks away.

She calls out weakly, "Happy Valentine's Day!"

I've been dreading Valentine's Day. "Quick," I say, tugging on Aviva's arm. "Give me your sunglasses. And your coat. And your scarf."

We stop by the lockers, and Aviva unpeels her layers. "Are you incognito?" she asks me as she slings her messenger bag over her shoulder and we keep walking.

"Yes. I'm hiding from Johann," I tell her. "It's Valentine's Day, and I'm hiding from my boyfriend because I'm scared he'll do something romantic."

"Does Johann usually do romantic stuff?" Aviva asks.

"Not really," I tell her. "I mean, he holds doors for me when we go out. And he pays for dinner. And once he gave me his sweater when I was cold. But I guess that stuff is more polite than romantic."

"Has he kissed you yet?"

I shake my head.

"Hug?" Aviva asks.

"Not even a handshake," I tell her.

"So you have nothing to worry about," Aviva says. "I doubt he's gonna suddenly get romantic today and whip out his piccolo and serenade you in the hallway."

"Ugh," I say. "Don't even say that. Don't put that idea out in the universe."

"It won't happen," Aviva reassures me, and then grins. "A little man in clogs playing a teeny tiny flute is *waaaay* more Saint Patrick's Day than Valentine's."

My disguise is pointless, because Johann is nowhere to be seen. Hunter is, though—hanging out in his usual doorway spot with Derek.

"Hey, Hunter," I say to him, after I give Aviva back her sunglasses.

"*Heyyyy*," Hunter drawls back, with his slow smile.

Out of nowhere, Diva comes barreling toward us and jumps on Hunter, slamming his head back into the lockers.

"Whoa," Hunter says into Diva's face, which is an inch away from his.

"*Happy Valentine's Day!*" Diva screeches.

Then she kisses him.

The rest of the day goes by and I don't bump into Johann once. At some point I realize that it's probably because he's avoiding me, too. I'm sure he has no clue how to act on Valentine's Day, between the fact that he's never had a girlfriend before and the awkward sham of a relationship that we have. Just as I let myself start to feel really lonely, I hear raised voices in the hallway.

"I can't believe you took my prom date to Burger King!" Pam yells at Amy. Then, before Amy can answer, Pam turns to Josh and says, "I can't believe you went to Burger King with her!"

Julius seniors are allowed to go out to lunch, and Amy and Josh just came in from the parking lot in their big coats with Burger King bags in their hands. They were stomping the snow off their boots when Pam came up to confront them.

"*Whaa...*" Josh begins, but Pam rips the greasy bag out of his hand, and then he whines, "What the hell? I need that Whopper. I'm starving."

"He's your prom date, not your boyfriend," Amy tells

Pam, rolling her eyes, tired of Pam's tantrums. "We just went to lunch together. Nothing happened."

"Yeah, nothing happened," Josh echoes.

"What?" Pam looks up at Josh like he's an idiot. "No! I don't care what you two do. Go make out. I don't care."

She turns to Amy. "But *do not* take my prom date to Burger King. He's gonna weigh five thousand pounds by the time we take our prom pictures. I did not give Eugene two hundred euros to import me a pair of French Spanx so I could take professional pictures next to a bloated, greasy doofus."

Poor Josh. Pam just called him fat and ran away with his lunch, and now Amy won't share her fries with him. I guess someone is having a worse Valentine's Day than I am.

When I get to the chem room for double lab period with Hunter, he doesn't say anything about Valentine's Day or Diva. In fact, the class is totally normal until an announcement comes over the loudspeaker, letting us know that the school is conducting an emergency earthquake drill. Over the sound of everyone cheering that lab got interrupted, we hear our teacher Mr. Winther say something about taking cover under a table until the shaking stops. There's no shaking, but Derek jogs over to a desk and slides under it like he's sliding into second base. Eugene goes over to another desk, sighs, and lays the handkerchief he always carries on the ground, kneels under the desk, and starts texting on his BlackBerry. Hunter and I crawl under our lab table.

"My little sister, Lila, would be so excited about this," I

tell Hunter. "She loves natural disasters. She watches The Weather Channel all the time, and she's only seven."

Hunter laughs. "Sounds like she's gonna be one of those tornado-chasers one day. I'm clueless — I didn't even know we had earthquakes in Wisconsin."

I shake my head. "We'll probably never have one. They mostly happen at fault lines — like, where the plates of the earth meet each other. The plates shift, and everything gets shaken up."

"Wow." Hunter turns his head back to look at me. "You're an expert."

I laugh. "I had to learn enough to prove to Lila that we'll never have one."

Being this close to Hunter, I'm suddenly aware of his breath, and I start to feel nervous.

I have to ask. I have to know about him and Diva.

I say, "So this is how Julius celebrates Valentine's Day."

"Ughhhh," Hunter says with a sigh. His shoulders sink.

"What?"

"I don't know," Hunter says. "Valentine's Day is just so annoying."

He accidentally puts his left hand down on my right hand, balancing all his weight on me for a second.

"Sorry!" he says, and then continues. "No, like, probably Valentine's Day can be cool with someone you like. Like, are you and Johann doing something?"

"No," I say quickly. "I didn't even see him today."

"Diva wants me to buy her something," Hunter says.

"But I'm not. She's so annoying. She just, like, randomly told people we're dating."

"So you're not dating?"

I can feel my pulse in my throat.

"Nah. I dunno. I mean, I guess we are."

I lift my head and blurt out, "I don't even like Johann. I don't really know why we're going out."

I want Hunter to look relieved or excited. But instead he looks sympathetic. *Does he feel bad for me?*

"He's a nice guy, though," Hunter says.

"I just...He's...I don't like him like that," I say. I know I sound completely desperate, but I keep going. "I don't even know how we ended up going out."

Hunter smiles. "Well, I know how I ended up going out with Diva....I got drunk and passed out, and she took advantage of me."

We both laugh out loud. Hunter's eyes are so ridiculously blue, and I know that I'm staring at him for longer than I should, but he's looking at me, too. I'm scared to move any part of my body, including my eyes.

Hunter moves his hand, and it lands on mine again. This time he doesn't say sorry, and I don't want him to. Then he tilts his head, and I realize that he's about to kiss me....

And the loudspeaker crackles, and Hunter retreats, banging his head against the table.

"Thank you for participating in this emergency drill," Dr. Nicholas's voice booms over the loudspeaker. "Please resume your classes."

Mr. Winther picks up the discussion. "As I'm sure most of you realize, we did not have a real earthquake today. However..."

No, it wasn't a real earthquake. Nothing shifted today. But I have hope. There are definitely fault lines here.

CHAPTER 23: HUNTER

"Anonymous Senior Gives Tell-All Report About
Being Forced into Prom Contract"

"The Boy Recession©" by Aviva Roth,
The Julius Journal, February

I feel like shit.

Actually, I feel worse than shit. I feel like dog shit in a paper bag that Derek set on fire on someone's porch. My head hurts. My neck and shoulders hurt. I feel like I've been lifting weights, even though obviously I haven't. And I'm more tired than usual this week. Musical rehearsals have been wearing me out, but this is a different kind of tired. I'm just dragging my ass around. I don't even have the energy to pretend I'm not sleeping in class.

"Hunter, you are *super*-sweaty," Diva tells me.

"I'm aware," I say. "And I can't breathe. Can you get offa me?"

She's sitting on my lap, because we just finished this song, "We Both Reached for the Gun," where I pretend to be a puppet master and she's a puppet. The spotlights are really bothering me, and Diva's weight on my legs is making my thighs go numb. I push her off, and she lands on her ass on the stage and whines, "Hunter!"

Pulling my sticky T-shirt away from my chest, I stand up and start to walk offstage. I need to get out of these spotlights. But before I get to the stairs, Mrs. Martin calls out from her seat in the front row of the audience.

"Billy Flynn!" she says. "Let's take those last few measures again."

I trudge back toward the chair, which Diva's sitting in now.

"Can we do it without her in my lap?" I say. "She's heavy. My legs are all sore."

"Hunter!" Diva whines again.

"Get back into position," Mrs. Martin says. "She is the puppet; you are pulling the strings. All of your body movements must be coordinated. And she must be mouthing the words at the same time you are singing the words. You must be completely attuned to each other."

"I don't know if I should even sing any more," I say, squinting out at Mrs. Martin with my hand up to shade my eyes. "My throat is sore."

"If your throat is sore, you are not singing properly," Mrs. Martin says. "You should not be singing from your throat. You should be singing from your *diaphragm*."

"I'm singing the right way," I snap. "I know how to sing. My throat isn't sore because I'm singing. My throat is sore, so I don't wanna sing."

"Sit down, Billy Flynn!"

Diva stands up next to the chair and crosses her arms to show she's pissed. When I'm in the chair and she lands on me with her full body weight again, I let out this involuntary grunt.

"Jesus Christ, Hunter," she hisses, without even looking back at me. "Get over yourself."

The piano guy starts the music, and Diva gets going with her puppet movements. Her arms are flinging and flailing all over the place, and she keeps hitting me in the face with her stupid elbows. I can't wait for this crap to be over.

When we finish the song, I push Diva off me again and head for the stairs, but Pam pops her head out of the stage curtains. She's got her headset on, and she calls out, "Billy Flynn! Where are you going? You have a costume fitting!"

"What?" I'm on the first step. "I can't do it tonight. I'm sweaty as hell."

"Oh, *you're* sweaty?" Pam says, holding up her clipboard. "I just hauled twelve boxes of dusty-ass costumes off a sketchy-ass truck and unpacked every single one of them to find the so-called pimp suit that you don't even deserve. So I think you can expend the energy to try on a pair of pants."

I'm too tired to fight with Pam. So I go into the auditorium, where they're fitting the costumes. I take off my pants in front of, like, ten people, and don't even care. Pam puts the suit pants on me and starts sticking pins or needles or something all up and down them. I'm standing, feeling dizzy, and my body's heating up like a generator.

"Can I sit down?" I ask Pam. "I don't feel well."

Diva is next to me, trying on her costume, and she looks over and rolls her eyes.

"You don't *feel* well? Seriously, Hunter?" she says. "Man up."

Man up? Pam actually lets me sit down, and the whole time she's busy fitting my jacket, I'm thinking about how much I hate Diva. Hatred is rare for me. But my girlfriend — I definitely hate her. She's gone from telling me what to wear to criticizing everything I wear and criticizing everything I do. I would dump her right now if I could do it without her screaming at me for three hours.

I almost kissed Kelly the other day. I would have done it, too. But we got interrupted when the emergency drill ended. But really I should have just kissed her the second we got under the table. I should have kissed her months ago. But now instead I'm stuck with Diva, and Kelly is dating Johann. Kelly is awesome and funny — and *nice*, which, I'm realizing more and more from spending time with Diva, Pam, Amy, and Mrs. Martin, is a really rare thing in a girl. I knew she was awesome and funny and nice, but I didn't do anything about it, because I'm lazy and stupid and a fucking slacker. I didn't ask her out back then, and I didn't kiss her the other day, and now I'm screwed and I have no one to blame but my own lazy ass.

The more I think about this, the worse I feel. I'm all

pissed at myself, sweaty, and my whole body hurts. Then I remember Kelly's hand. It's the weirdest thing, but when we were under that lab table, my hand was on top of her hand, and her hand was small and soft, and it felt really cool. Now I imagine her touching my forehead, smoothing my sweaty hair back with her palm, sliding her hand down my face and my neck. I'm thinking about it so hard that I can almost feel her hand. It's like those guys dying of thirst in the desert who see water and try to drink it even though it's really sand.

"Ow! What the crap?" I say, jumping off the chair.

"Did I stick you?" Pam asks. She's holding pins between her teeth.

"Yeah! The needle is still in there! Get it out!"

That's it. I'm done with this shit. I rip the jacket off and leave it on the chair. Pam tries to protest through the pins in her mouth, but I don't even look at her. I unzip my suit pants and let them drop to the floor.

"Hunter, what the hell?" Diva whines.

I pull on my jeans and then I take off, running down the stairs and into the audience. Actually, I'm trying to run, but my body's so weak that I'm actually jogging slowly. But I'm getting out of here.

Mrs. Martin looks up from the orchestra pit and calls out, "Billy Flynn!"

A girl in the audience says, "Hunter, your coat and your backpack are here," as I pass her going up the aisle.

But I ignore both of them and jog to the auditorium

door and plow into it, and even though I'm weak as hell, it bangs open really loudly. My fever is making me crazy, and I imagine I'm running to Kelly and that she'll be nice to me and touch me with her cool hands and not tell me to "man up" when I've got a nine-hundred-degree fever. But I realize I'm just running to anything that's cold that will cool me off.

So it's a good thing I live in Wisconsin, because we have a lot of cold stuff lying around everywhere. Once I get outside, I stand for a minute to feel the cold air blow against my sweaty skin and to breathe in the fresh air. Then I walk over to the side of the building and stick my face in a huge pile of snow.

CHAPTER 24: HUNTER

"He Had It Coming:
Chicago's Violent Female Leads Too
Familiar for Comfort?"

"The Boy Recession©" by Aviva Roth,
The Julius Journal, March

So, after three hours waiting around in the ER and two blood tests, I found out I've got mono.

When I stormed out of that rehearsal, I felt pretty badass. But then I realized I didn't have my phone or a ride, and I couldn't walk home because it was four degrees outside and I was in a T-shirt. So I had to sneak back inside to grab my stuff, and then sit out on the curb, waiting for my dad to pick me up. My doctor's office was closed, so my dad drove me to Columbia St. Mary's hospital in Milwaukee. Apparently doctors can't give you medicine to get rid of mono; you just have to rest for a few weeks and hope it goes away. The ER doctor warned me that mono makes you so tired you sleep ten or fifteen hours a night, which made me wonder, *How long have I had mono for?* I've been trying to sleep ten or fifteen hours a night since puberty.

So except for feeling shitty and sweating my ass off, being sick is pretty sweet. I get to stay in bed all day. No school. No homework. No musical practice. It's awesome. I get to sleep until three in the afternoon and have my mom tell me, "Good for you! Rest up!"

When I first disappeared from rehearsal, Diva freaked out and tried calling me five hundred times. As soon as I got out of the ER, I texted her *Got mono, can't talk, can't rehearse. Tell Mrs. Martin*, and then shut my phone off.

Apparently Diva spread the word about me being diseased pretty fast, because Eugene found out and called my house that same night. He let me know that Diva had been writing Facebook status updates on my "condition":

My poor boo is still home with swollen lymph nodes!

At rehearsal, missing my Billy Flynn! Rest up for opening night, boo!

My boo is starting to get better.... Get strong, boo!

Her updates are ridiculous, considering she has no clue what's going on with my lymph nodes or me. I refuse to text her or pick up her calls, and she refuses to visit me because she's scared she'll catch mono and miss the musical. But Eugene has come to visit me a bunch, and I think that he thinks I'm dying. A few days ago he brought rosary beads and spoke to me really seriously.

"How are you feeling, Huntro?" he asked me in this low voice.

"Why are you whispering?"

"You're sick!"

"I'm fine," I told him. "I'm just sleeping all day."

"Huntro, this mono is serious stuff," Eugene said. "Can the doctors do anything?"

"Not really."

"Oh my God!" Eugene sprung up from the chair in surprise and brought a fist up to his mouth.

"No, no!" I sat up in bed. "Like, they don't *have* to do anything. I just have to sleep for a while and it will get better."

"Huntro," Eugene said, sitting down again and leaning forward. "Your illness has got me thinking about my own mortality. Seriously, man. I've started writing my will. And I've decided I'm leaving Bobbi ten thousand dollars."

"What the hell?" I said.

"I know she and I aren't dating anymore," Eugene told me. "But finding all these people prom dates has made me think about love and compatibility. . . . I regret losing her. I do. I know we had our differences, with her being a Christian, and me being somewhat morally . . . ambivalent . . . but I really care about Bobbi. I want to take care of her, even if I catch your mono and die."

"No, I meant, like, what the hell?" I interrupted him.

"I'm the one who's sick, and you're trying to have a heart-to-heart about *you* right now? I have to listen to your dumb ass blabber on all the time — give *me* ten thousand dollars."

After that visit, Eugene felt bad, so he did me a bunch of favors. He went and told Mrs. Martin that I was on my death-bed and couldn't come to rehearsal. He started bringing me messages from school — homework from my teachers that I threw out right away, desperate pleas from George, who had to take my place as Billy Flynn and was going nuts from dealing with Diva. Today I'm lying in bed, feeling pretty great about not being Billy Flynn, when my dad yells up the stairs, "Hunter! Wake up, champ! You have a visitor!"

I hear someone coming up the stairs and I figure it's Eugene again, so I keep playing BrickBreaker on my phone and call out, "You got death threats or rosary beads today, gingerbread boy?"

But it's not Eugene — it's Diva. She stomps really loudly into my room, wearing a big coat that looks like it's made out of a dead bear. I wonder what made her finally decide to risk her precious lymph nodes to visit me.

"Hello, Hunter," Diva says. "How are you feeling?"

"Uh … okay," I say cautiously.

"Oh, so you feel *okay* about cheating on me?" Diva says, putting her hand on her hip.

What the hell? Is this girl delusional? Diva stomps the snow off her leather bitch boots and says, "I know about Kelly Robbins."

"How do you know about that?"

"Two people in school have mono," Diva informs me. "You are one of them, and Kelly is the other."

"How did she get it?" I ask, genuinely confused.

The look on Diva's face says, *Are you a complete moron?*

"So, what, are you *denying* it now? You're denying you guys hooked up? I don't get it, Hunter."

I start to tell her that nothing happened, but then I realize something: *This is my way out.* Sure, this girl is looming over me like she's Godzilla and I'm a flimsy Japanese building, but I always knew this breakup would be violent, and I gotta do it sometime. This time is as good as any. "Uh, no," I say. "I guess I'm not denying it."

"We are over," Diva tells me. "We are completely over. And don't think about coming crawling back to me. I don't want your gross disease."

Swinging her hair, Diva stomps out of my room, calling over her shoulder, "I'm never speaking to you again. Except for when I have to, in the musical."

Once she's gone, this huge weight lifts off my shoulders. I don't have a girlfriend anymore. I can wear whatever color shirt I want. I can walk down the hallway at school without getting harassed. I'm free.

And it was Kelly who set me free. Kelly *was* my escape. I could kiss that girl. And ya know what? I will kiss that girl. As soon as I get back to school, I'm gonna grab her, and I'm gonna kiss her.

CHAPTER 25: KELLY

*"Mono Mystery:
Connect the Cough Drops to See
Who's Been Kissing Whom"*

Special Graphics Edition of "The Boy Recession©"
by Aviva Roth, *The Julius Journal*, March

So does Diva still hate me?" I ask, propping myself up in bed with a bunch of pillows and stuffed animals my little sister, Lila, lent me to make me feel better.

This is my second sick visit from Darcy and Aviva. When they came over last week, Darcy was wearing a surgical mask and wouldn't come past the doorway. But over the weekend she did some research and found out I can only give it to her if she shares my toothbrush or lip gloss or kisses me. So today she's actually in my room, organizing homework assignments for me. Aviva brought me a chai tea latte from Starbucks ("This counts as fluids, right?"). This is why I need two best friends.

"I think she's toned down the hostility a little bit," Aviva says, curling up on the foot of my bed. "Here, let me check my phone.... Okay, her last Tweet about you was a whole twelve hours ago. That's progress!"

"What was it?"

"'Still hating that diseased hussy,'" Aviva says. "Oh, and there's a sad face, too."

"But she doesn't have mono yet?" I ask hopefully.

"I wish," Aviva says. "It gives you a sore throat, right? Maybe if she got it, she would shut up for a few days. Or give up singing."

"No one else has mono yet?"

"No one else. Just you and Hunter," Darcy says from my desk, where she's rubbing antibacterial gel into her hands. "It's so weird. It's actually ironic. You know what you have? Ironic mono."

"I know, I know."

"It really is ironic!" Darcy continues, fascinated. "I mean, you got mono, but you didn't even get kissed!"

"I know," I snap.

"But you did have that almost-kiss," Aviva says. "Which I still don't understand, by the way. What is an almost-kiss?"

I must have explained what happened between Hunter and me under the lab table five times, but Aviva still doesn't get it. She pulls her knitting out of her giant purse—she heard the actors from *Gossip Girl* were knitting one another scarves, and she decided to knit me a get-well one—and waits for an explanation.

"I told you we just had that moment *before* a kiss. You

know, you're looking at each other, and you know it's about to happen."

Aviva shakes her head. "I don't think I ever had that moment. I usually dive-bomb them."

I sigh and slump back into my pillow pile. I hate being sick. I've been out of school for only four days, and I already feel like I'm behind on everything. On top of that, there's the Hunter situation. Diva is going around school telling people I stole her boyfriend, but I didn't steal him. If I stole him, I would actually have him.

"But the ironic mono was actually *good*!" Darcy says. "The ironic mono broke up Hunter and Diva. He's single now, thanks to the mono. And you're single now, too."

That's true. I am single—Johann and I broke up in the nurse's office the day I got mono. I had been feeling bad all day, and finally Johann convinced me to go to the nurse's office. He stayed with me while I waited to get my temperature taken, and I felt so sick and also guilty about not really liking a nice guy like Johann. Finally I started to cry, and poor Johann was totally bewildered. When I pulled myself together, I didn't know how to explain what was wrong. Everything seemed wrong.

"You're so nice," I began, between my gasps. "You're so nice to sit here when I'm sick, and gross, and..."

"It's okay." Johann shrugged and patted my arm.

"Don't.... You don't have to touch me," I told Johann apologetically, as I shifted loudly against the really noisy crinkly paper on the nurse's exam table.

"Um, Kelly?" Johann said. "Do you think we...Do you think we should be really going out? It's just...every time I touch you or anything, you tell me not to."

"No, I don't!" I protested.

But what he was saying was true.

"I feel bad that you've been sick so much," Johann continued. "But maybe we should...I don't know, do you think you should just focus on getting better for now?"

Always the gentleman, Johann was even considerate while he was dumping me. Even now, a week later, I feel guilty and awkward when I think about him.

"You *are* single!" Aviva realizes, looking up from her very tangled knitting. "*Ooh*, you should ask Hunter to the prom!"

"The prom?" I say. "There's still snow on the ground! Isn't it a little early?"

"Not according to the female population of Julius," Darcy says, rolling her eyes. "You've been missing the mass panic that started last week. A few girls got dates, and then everyone without a date got freaked out. Pam is selling copies of her prom contract. And Kristin Chung asked *George!*"

"Ew!" I gasp in horror.

The whole time she's talking, Darcy's also writing on yellow Post-its, filling them up with homework assignments and tips on lessons that I've missed.

"It's ridiculous. I've been trying to do the Women's History Month agenda in student senate, but the prom committee updates take up forty-five minutes every week. The whole meeting dissolves into people whining about not having dates and fighting over dates! I have to buy a gavel. Or some pepper spray."

Darcy's next Post-it has PEPPER SPRAY written on it in huge letters.

"Darcy just has no sympathy," Aviva tells me. "Because she has a date."

"What's this?" I ask, sitting up and sipping my chai tea.

At my desk, Darcy is shaking her head. "I do not have a date. I have an offer, which I'm going to refuse."

"Derek Palewski." Aviva grins at me over her knitting needles.

"Darcy, he is your husband," I tease. "The least you could do is take him to the prom."

"No way. He doesn't meet any of my requirements. He smokes. He has, like, nine body piercings. He wears flip-flops when he's not at the beach. He doesn't have a 4.0 GPA or a 401(k)."

Aviva rolls her eyes. "Darcy, no one can live up to those standards."

"Viva, who are you taking?" I ask.

Picking up a stitch, Aviva says casually, "I'm thinking about getting a prostitute."

I look over at Darcy. "If most people told me that, I would be surprised."

Darcy rolls her eyes. "It's not technically prostitution. Eugene's setting people up with prom dates for money."

"Who are these dates? Julius guys?"

"No, no," Aviva says. "He's got a good selection! He's got private-school guys, college guys, this big basketball star from Milwaukee.... He's got a whole binder full of guys, with head shots and everything. The boy binder. He let me peek at it. He said he's not done recruiting, though."

"Did you see someone you liked?"

"I don't have to *like* him," Aviva informs me. "I'm a career girl. I'm just using him for my article: 'My Night with a Prom-stitute.' Can you think of a catchier title than that?"

"Um..."

"I should snatch one up soon, though," Aviva says. "Remind me to put my deposit down on a hot date. Here, Darce, gimme a Post-it."

"So lots of people have dates already?" I ask. "Do you think someone will ask Hunter?"

"Not if you ask him first," Aviva says.

"Do you want my phone?" Darcy asks, standing up to deliver Aviva's Post-it.

Aviva scribbles DATE on it, and then sticks it on her own forehead.

"You can call him right now and ask him."

"I can't call him," I say. "He's in bed with mono, and he just got dumped."

"Exactly!" Darcy says. "Perfect timing."

"I'll look completely desperate!"

"But he likes you," Aviva says, looking at me from under her Post-it. "He almost kissed you."

"I don't know. I think I need to ask Hunter in person," I say. "I need to feel him out first, read his body language, and see how he feels about the whole Diva thing before I ask him."

"So ask him when he gets better," Darcy says.

"But what if *he* gets better before *I* get better, and he shows up at school, and someone asks him?"

"They could," Aviva acknowledges. "He looks a lot better since that haircut."

"Yeah, no one would have asked him with his old hair," Darcy says. "They wouldn't have even been able to find him. He was like the yeti."

I moan and put my hand on my forehead, which is really hot.

"It will be fine!" Darcy says.

"Yeah. If he gets back and a girl tries to talk to him, Darce and I will run interference," Aviva says. "We'll hip-check her into the lockers."

"But hopefully we won't have to," Darcy says, glaring at Aviva. "Seeing as we could get *suspended* for that. *Hopefully*, Kelly will rest up and get better by the time Hunter gets better."

"He got mono first," I say doubtfully. "He has a week head start on me."

"It's a race!" Darcy says. "And you're going to win.

You're going to get fluids, take Advil, and rest. And you're going to win."

"A mono race?" I say, raising one eyebrow.

"That's gonna be the slowest race," Aviva says, "since the tortoise and the tortoise."

CHAPTER 26: HUNTER

"Billy Flynn and the Boys:
Meet the Men of This Year's Musical"

"The Boy Recession©" by Aviva Roth,
The Julius Journal, March

It's the first night of *Chicago*, and Eugene is patting me down in one of the band practice rooms.

"Okay, I think you're ready," he says. "You've got your suit. You've got your vest. You've got your cravat. You've got your stickpin. You've got your cuff links. You've got your pocket square. Did I forget anything?"

"No clue. I don't know what half of that stuff is," I tell him as he kneels down to pull my pants down over my dress shoes. While Eugene's shining my shoe with his handkerchief, I look at his watch and realize there's only a half-hour until the show starts. Have I really been getting dressed for, like, twenty minutes?

"This took forever," I say. "How do stylish dudes put all this stuff on every day?"

Eugene stands up and sighs, putting his handkerchief back in his pocket.

"It's a real burden on us," he says.

I look down.

"Don't you think these are kinda tight?" I ask Eugene, pulling the fly of the pants away from my crotch.

"This is how clothes fit, Huntro," Eugene informs me. "You're a man, not a scarecrow."

"I guess."

Eugene opens the practice room's door and runs out to grab a mirror. When he comes back and holds it up to me, I whistle.

"Holy crap," I say. "I look like that douchebag who's dating the other Kardashian sister."

"Don't hate on Scott Disick," Eugene warns me. "He's my fashion role model."

My hair has a crapload of gel in it, so it looks wet, but when I touch it, it feels all crunchy. You can see the comb marks going through it, in perfect lines, and Pam slathered makeup all over my face. But the suit actually looks good.

"Hmmm."

Eugene isn't totally satisfied. He's tapping his finger against his chin.

"Aha! I know what you're missing," he says, and takes off his huge bling-bling watch and puts it on my wrist. "The final touch," he says, and we go out into the band room.

It's total chaos in here, because the entire cast is getting ready. All the chorus girls are running around, crashing into one another like bumper cars, and Pam is screaming at them, "Stop running around! Your sequins are falling off! You're losing sequins! *Freeze! Freeze!*"

"So," Eugene says, "how ya feelin'?"

"Uh…" I look around at the craziness and laugh.

"No, I mean, how's the mono?"

"Oh, I'm okay," I say. "I'm pretty much healthy, I guess."

I got back to school last week, in time for final dress rehearsals, and it's been totally fine. I know my lines. I know the dances. I'm good to go. It was actually lucky I was out for all that time, because it gave Mrs. Martin a chance to teach Diva how to sing. Well, sort of. Right now Diva's over by the piano, doing vocal warm-ups. I feel really bad for the piano guy—she's shouting in his ear.

"You're not gonna pass out or anything?" Eugene asks me.

"I'm pretty sweaty in all these layers," I say, unbuttoning my jacket over my vest. "But I think I'll be good."

"What about your ulcer?" Eugene says. "You got that ulcer again?"

"What, do you *want* me to be sick?" I ask him.

"I'm just letting you know I'm here for you!" Eugene says, raising his hands innocently. "I've got Pepto-Bismol, and I'm here for you."

"No ulcer tonight," I tell him. "I'm ready to go out there and kick ass. I have strong motivation to nail this thing."

"What?"

I point to Diva.

"I wanna be so good that everyone's watching me instead of her," I tell Eugene. "Because when people don't give her attention, she gets super pissed off."

Just as I say this, Diva crosses the room to come bother me and Eugene. She's got this crazy wig that Pam duct-taped to her head. Crooked.

"You're supposed to be warming up your voice," she tells me.

"I couldn't. You were at the piano forever."

"Well, I'm *obviously* not at the piano anymore."

"Okay. I'll go in a minute."

That should be the end of the conversation. But Diva feels the need to hover around and wait for me to say something to her. I don't, so she says, "I saw what you wrote in the program. And it was really, really stupid."

Last week we were supposed to write biographies of ourselves for the musical's program. I wrote: "This performance is for All the Young Dudes." That's it. One line. "All the Young Dudes" is this Mott the Hoople song that was actually written by David Bowie. I love Bowie, and I friggin' love that song. So I put that in there, because what the hell.

"No one even knows what that means," Diva tells me.

"I know what it means," I say, leaning against the bandstand railing. "Seventies-music aficionados know what it means. Eugene knows what it means."

Eugene, on his BlackBerry, holds up his hand.

"Leave me out of this," he says.

"Ugh. You guys are so annoying. I'm so glad I don't have to hang out with you anymore."

"Yeah," I say, rebuttoning my jacket. "Ditto."

"You should go warm up your voice," Diva says. "You need it."

I don't want to fight with Diva, but she keeps trying to start crap with me, and so I've decided that I'm ready to upstage her ass in this show. As I enter the backstage area and look over in the wings, I see my dad holding a program and my Al Capone–style gangster hat. "You left this in the car," he tells me. "Wow! Look at this place!"

By now, people are throwing clothes, tripping over one another, and practicing dance moves one last time. Mrs. Martin's trying to yell over all the noise, but she starts hacking up a lung.

"It's great back here!" my dad tells me. "So much energy!"

"Uh, yeah. I guess."

"This reminds me of my swim team state championships, the year I was captain," my dad says. "There was such great energy. So much team spirit."

"Yeah," I say, watching Pam chase George down with her hot glue gun. "Team spirit."

"Man, this is so exciting, champ," my dad tells me, clapping a hand on my shoulder. "Isn't it so great, being part of a team? Not only part of the team—you're a *leader* tonight. Everyone depending on you...It's such a great feeling. Remember this, Hunter."

I stop tugging on the crotch of my pants, because I realize this is a pretty important moment for my dad. Sure, he's kinda living vicariously through me, because he loved the good old days when he was an athlete...or the good old days when he had a job...but he's probably right. I've got a big part tonight, and that's a cool thing; I should live up to it.

"I'm proud of you, man," my dad says, and hugs me before he leaves.

"Ten minutes, everyone! Ten minutes to curtain!" Mrs. Martin yells, and all the chorus girls start screaming.

"If you have to pee, you better pee *now!*" Pam adds.

As I go back over to the piano for my warm-up, I'm thinking *Oh, crap.* I wasn't nervous at all when I was gunning for a kick-ass performance to get revenge on Diva. But now that I want to rock this Billy Flynn thing because all these people are depending on me, and because my dad's so amped to see me onstage, I think I feel that ulcer again. *Damn. Where'd Eugene go with the Pepto?*

CHAPTER 27: KELLY

*"Is Theater the New Football?
The Men of Julius Embrace the Arts"*

"The Boy Recession©" by Aviva Roth,
The Julius Journal, March

He was really, really good!" Aviva says in my ear, so I can hear her over everyone's applause. "I don't even have to lie in my review!"

It's my first time back at Julius since I got mono, and Hunter's getting a standing ovation.

"Plus, he's dressed a lot better than he was at Open-Mic Night," Aviva says. "I think he read my advice in the newspaper."

"Viva, that's his *costume*," I tell her, without taking my eyes off the stage.

After a quick bow, Hunter backs up into the crowd of other cast members. But the director, Mrs. Martin, grabs his arm and forces him to take another bow, because we're still standing and clapping for him. Diva, who already took a bow, takes a few steps forward, like she's waiting for her turn for a standing ovation. But she didn't get one before, and she's not gonna get one now. This is all for Hunter.

When the show first began, I barely recognized him. It wasn't just the costume. All the usual Hunter habits were gone; instead, he was Billy Flynn. He was loud and assertive and arrogant. He spread his arms out when he talked, and when other people talked, he drew attention to himself by stroking the lapels of his suit, flashing his shiny cuff links, and pulling up his sleeve to show off a giant, sparkly watch. He kept checking out chorus girls with an exaggerated up-and-down look, and when he made a joke, he would turn to us — the audience — and wink. Even his singing was different tonight; he had this quick, staccato way with the lyrics, the complete opposite of his usual drawling voice.

"I'm going backstage," I tell Aviva.

"Do it! Do it!" Aviva says, bouncing up and down in excitement. "I'll watch your coat."

Usually I would need lots of encouragement before going backstage, but tonight I feel different.

I hurry up the aisle of the auditorium, push open the doors, and go down the main hallway toward the east hallway. I duck into the band room, which has been completely taken over by the cast. There are racks of costumes and tables covered with lipsticks and makeup compacts everywhere. I push open the door to the stage, and I'm blinded by camera flashes. There are even more people than there were the last time I was backstage — parents with big bouquets of flowers, yearbook staff taking pictures, crew dressed in black, and the cast members in their freaky makeup. Onstage they looked normal, but up close, they're scary. The girls all have cracked bright red clown lips and blue eye shadow up to their eyebrows, and the boys have orange foundation smeared all over their faces and necks, and black eyeliner that looks like permanent marker.

"Look who it is. Typhoid Mary." Diva is coming toward me, in her super-high stage heels. "Looks like you're feeling better," she says.

When Darcy and Aviva first told me Diva hated me, I was really upset. People never hate me. It bugged me so much I thought about sending her a Facebook message explaining I didn't hook up with Hunter. I even thought about using Darcy's research to prove you can get mono other ways than kissing, but I didn't think Diva would feel any better about her boyfriend using my toothbrush or my lip gloss.

Now that she's confronting me, though, I actually feel kind of excited. You're supposed to get in at least one fight in high school, right?

"I am feeling better," I say, and smile.

Diva doesn't smile back.

"Thank you for spreading your disgusting mono around to my boyfriend," she says in a hoarse whisper. "I really appreciate it. You broke me and Hunter up, *and* you almost ruined the show. If I got sick because of you, my agent would have sued you."

"Yeah, that would have been a real shame," I say. "If you got sick and missed the show. No one would have heard your *beautiful* voice."

It takes Diva a second to register my sarcasm; when she does, she gets ready to start screeching, but just then Amy's mom interrupts us.

"Congratulations! You were wonderful!" Amy's mom says.

Diva turns around and gushes in a sweet voice, "Oh my gosh, thank you!" and they hug.

A minute later, Diva turns back to me and says, "You act like a big kiss-ass, you act like you're so nice to everybody, and then you go and steal my boyfriend. You are so fake. You are so ridiculously... Oh my God, are those for me? Oh my God, I *love* you!"

A junior spandexer appears with flowers for Diva, and she flips immediately from I-hate-Kelly mode to I-love-flowers mode. Taking this as my chance to escape, I turn to look for Hunter.

But I don't need to, because Hunter is pushing forward to find me.

When we meet in the crowd, he wraps his long arms around me, pulls me against his sweat-soaked suit, and holds me there longer than a normal hug. My ear is against his chest, I'm warm and close, and I think Hunter smells good, no matter what Darcy says about his hygiene. When he pulls away, his orangey makeup smears against my forehead. Hunter cups my temple with his hand and rubs the makeup smudge on my forehead with his thumb.

"I'm getting makeup all over you," he says.

"Oh, don't worry," I say. "Guys do that to me all the time."

I'm pretty sure the makeup smudge is gone, but his hand is still on my face, and he looks at me intently.

"Will you go to the prom with me?" I ask him.

"Yeah!" Hunter says right away with a smile. "Hell, yeah!"

"Okay!" I say.

"Okay! Yeah! Cool!"

Hunter realizes he's talking in exclamation points, laughs at himself, and shakes his head. That one piece of hair falls across his face.

"Okay!" I say again, laughing.

"It was 'cause you saw me in the suit, right?" Hunter says. "Eugene always told me to dress up, and I never listened. I coulda been getting girls this whole time."

"It was definitely the suit," I tell him. "I love the stickpin."

I reach out and touch the pin that's glittering on his tie.

"I thought I was gonna stab myself this whole time," Hunter says. "But if you like it, I can get one for the tux...."

"*Cast photo!*" Mrs. Martin shouts, and someone pulls Hunter away.

All the cast members from the show go out onto the

stage and try to get close enough so the whole huge group fits in the picture. The three leads—Hunter, Diva, and Amy—pose in the front with their arms around one another. For one of the pictures, Mrs. Martin yells out, "Girls, kiss him! Kiss Billy Flynn!" So in the next picture, Diva and Amy, on either side of Hunter, are each kissing him on the cheek.

But seeing him with other girls is different this time. This time, I don't feel jealous.

CHAPTER 28: HUNTER

"Aviva's Sneak Peek:
Your Preview of the Hottest Escorts
in the Boy Binder"

"The Boy Recession©" by Aviva Roth,
The Julius Journal, April

Yesterday was April Fools' Day, so when Eugene called me up and asked me to come help lift up his boat, I thought he was screwing around. But here I am—Saturday, ten o'clock in the friggin' morning, and I'm at the marina.

The musical is over, so life is pretty much back to normal. Right after the show, things were different. My teachers congratulated me, and when my dad dropped me off in the morning, all these parents rolled down their windows and told me that I was an awesome Billy Flynn. And on the bulletin board in the main hallway, there were all these pictures of the cast. But then yesterday April rolled around, and they took the *Chicago* pictures down and put up this weird display that said: "A Parent's Guide to Sniffing: Spring Allergies or Drug Use?" That's how I knew my fifteen minutes of fame were up.

So now I'm back to my normal stuff—driving around with Derek, Dave, and Damian, hanging out at the gas station, chilling out at my house, playing video games, sleeping in on weekends—except today. This morning Eugene was honking under my window at 9:45 AM, forcing me out of bed. He and Derek borrowed a truck from his neighbor to hitch up his old-ass rusty boat trailer.

"How'd he get you to do this?" I ask Derek as we stand out on the dock, waiting for Eugene to start bossing us around.

The wind off the lake is whipping through my pajama pants—yeah, I'm still wearing my pajamas. Derek's got the hood of his sweatshirt up, and he's trying to block the wind with his hand to light a cigarette. He fails, gives up, and chucks the thing into the water.

"Promised me a hundred bucks," Derek says. "What about you?"

"He's giving me some valuable advice," I say, looking out at the water.

"Stock tip?"

I shake my head. *"Nahhh."*

Eugene backs the truck up as close to the dock as he can get. Then he stops it, hops out, and slams the door behind him.

"Great spring day to be out on the water!" he says, coming at us and rubbing his hands together.

"Yeah, gotta love the windchill," I say. "Remember, I've kinda still got mono."

"You'll be fine," Eugene says. "This will be a piece of cake! I'll be backing the truck up, and you guys make sure the trailer stays in the middle of the dock. Lemme know if I need to go left or right, and lemme know when I gotta stop. Once I stop, you guys unhitch the trailer. Then we get the boat off, slide that baby into the water, and, bada-bing, bada-boom, we're floating."

The way Eugene explains it, it sounds easy and almost fun. But as soon as we get started, we realize it's not easy or fun, and everything goes wrong. First Eugene reverses down the dock ramp at full speed, with Derek and me screaming at him, "Go right! Go right!" But of course he ignores us and doesn't go right, and the boat trailer starts to careen off the side of the dock. Derek has to jump into the cold-ass lake to keep the boat on track.

"Why the hell did you take this out of the water in the first place?" I ask Eugene as I struggle with the stupid rusty trailer hitch.

"The lake can freeze over, Huntro!"

"Everyone left their big yachts in there."

"If you leave your boat in the water, you have to winterize it," Eugene says. Even though it's his boat, he's not helping us with the hitch. He's standing at the top of the dock, "directing" us. "And I don't know how to winterize a boat."

"You don't know how to do this, either!" yells Derek, who's trying to brace his wet sneakers against the slippery dock.

I try to just grit my teeth and bear it, because Eugene has promised that the advice he's going to give me is pretty important.

"Okay, lay it on me," I tell Eugene a half-hour later, when we're out on the water. "Tell me how to be the perfect date."

We're hanging out on the boat, and Eugene has rewarded us with beers and snacks. It's actually not too cold now that the sun's out, but the beer has so much ice on it I'm holding it with my sleeve instead of my hand. Derek's lounging on the deck in the sun with a baseball hat over his face, drying off. He lifts his head up for a minute and squints at us to ask, "What is this? This is the advice you want?"

"Huntro's in love," Eugene informs Derek, shutting the top of the cooler and sitting down next to me.

"What? Nah," I say, leaning my head back against the railing.

"You are!" Eugene says. Then, to Derek, "He's in love. You know when I knew? Sunday night, soon as he's done the last show of *Chicago*, Hunter calls me up, asks me what a cummerbund is."

"Vegetable!" Derek guesses, like we're playing a trivia game.

We both ignore him.

"I'm not in love, dude. I just didn't know what a cummerbund was."

I'm not in love, but I'm totally pumped to go to the prom with Kelly. It's kinda funny—when I thought I'd have to go with Diva, I was dreading wearing a nice suit and paying for the limo and taking a million pictures. But now that I'm going with Kelly, I want to get an awesome suit, and pay for the limo, and take a million pictures. I'm determined to be a kick-ass date. In fact, I'm so determined to be a kick-ass date that I'm gonna listen to Eugene's advice, and take notes, and not make fun of him when he talks. That's a big sacrifice for me.

"The basic foundation of seduction is etiquette," Eugene says, standing up, taking off his sunglasses, and putting them in his pocket.

"Be a gentleman. When she walks in a room, you stand up. When she gets to a door, you open it. When she gets to a chair, you pull it out."

"Bullshit!" Derek calls out, his voice muffled by his hat. "Women can hold their own doors and pull out their own chairs. You're a sexist pig, Eugene."

"I don't give a crap how stupid Eugene sounds," I say. "When it comes to this stuff, I'm listening to him."

"Why?"

"Picture in your head what Bobbi looks like."

Derek lifts up his hat to show us that he's smirking. "I often do."

"Watch your mouth!" Eugene warns.

"Now, look at Eugene," I instruct Derek, extending my hand toward the captain of the vessel. "Observe the sweater vest and the chubby little sausage fingers. And remember this amazing fact: *He* dumped *her*."

Derek sits up and pushes his hat back. "Okay," he says. "I'm paying attention."

Eugene sits down to continue his lecture.

"A big romantic gesture can do a lot," he says. "And if it's a *surprise* big romantic gesture, you get double points. Like, Bobbi and I were going through her family photo album, and she showed me this necklace her grandpa gave her grandma after they came to America. I had a jeweler re-create it. But with a bigger stone, of course," Eugene adds proudly.

"Hold up," I say. "I don't have any money. I have, like, eight dollars in an empty pretzel tub."

"It's not about the money, Huntro," Eugene says, stepping over a bunch of ropes to go fix one of the sails. "It's about doing something personal, something that means something to the girl. What does Kelly like?"

I'm drinking from my Heineken, and I shrug.

"I dunno. She likes everything, I think. She's not Diva, so she's actually a nice person. . . . I dunno, music?"

"Okay, okay," Eugene says thoughtfully. "We can work with that. Lemme ruminate."

"Man, Huntro, I'm glad our prom dates are friends," Derek says. "We get to ride in the same limo."

I look over at Eugene and raise my eyebrows. Eugene, who's folding his handkerchief, just shakes his head.

"Uh...dude?" I say to Derek. "I thought Darcy turned you down."

"I'm gonna win her over," Derek says, standing up and resting his arm on the railing, totally confident. "Don't worry. She'll be my date."

"You gonna hold some doors and give her a necklace?"

Derek shakes his head. "I'm gonna tell her she has to bring me, to save me from a life of prostitution."

"What?"

"What? It's true, right?" Derek appeals to Eugene. "If I don't have a date, you're gonna force me into prostitution, right?"

"It's not prostitution!" Eugene says. "But yeah, I'd probably recruit you."

"See?" Derek says to me.

"What about you, gingerbread boy? You got a date? Or are you full-time pimp for the night?"

"Full-time pimp," Eugene says, sighing. "But I found out Bobbi was going alone. She and Diva are doing the independent-women thing. I should have asked her."

"You dumped her!" Derek says.

"We're still friends. And I think I miss her, guys. I *do* miss her. I do."

"Of course you do," Derek says. "You invested a crap-load of money in her. I mean, that necklace?" He whistles.

"No, not the necklace," Eugene says. "I don't care about the money. I mean, I'm trying to expense it on my tax return, but I don't care about the money. Or the promise-ring thing. I miss her. I miss hanging out with her. I was so comfortable with her. I could be myself."

"Your greedy, greasy self," I say, grinning.

But Eugene's words get me thinking. *I was so comfortable with her. I could be myself.* It actually reminds me of the song I wrote. As soon as I realize that, a plan for a romantic gesture starts forming in my head.

"Yo, Derek!" I call out.

While I was spacing out, Derek climbed onto the dock to tie up the boat. When he looks at me, I ask him, "You think you and the D-Bags could actually learn to play some music?"

CHAPTER 29: KELLY

"Faux-Feminists Burn Bras, Boycott Prom"

"The Boy Recession©" by Aviva Roth,
The Julius Journal, April

So the first-wave feminists were all about legal rights,"
Diva says. "They wanted to be allowed to vote, so they went
around with these axes, smashing up all the bars. At the
end of the night, it looked like an episode of *Bad Girls Club*.
Does anyone watch that, on Oxygen? Oxygen is a feminist
television network, by the way. So is Oprah's channel.

"So anyway, the reason we get to vote is because of
these women called suffragettes. The most famous suffrag-
ette was the mom from *Mary Poppins*. She showed us the
true meaning of feminism by leaving her children behind
and forgetting about them so she could go out and do political stuff...."

It's the second week in April, and I'm sitting through
Diva's U.S. history oral report on the Women's Rights
Movement. Somehow, while I was in bed with mono, our

class covered everything from the Great Depression to Reaganomics. Now I have to catch up, because our AP test is only a month away. These presentations we're doing this week are bearable only because there's finally sun coming through the classroom windows and it's warm enough that I'm not wearing a turtleneck sweater.

"What's the deal with this?" I whisper to Darcy, leaning across the aisle. "She's not making any sense, but she seems really into it."

You know that a presentation is bad when even Darcy isn't taking notes. She's sorting her pencils by size and color.

"She thinks she's a feminist," Darcy tells me. "It's her new obsession. She's moved on from hating you."

"…So when the third wave came around, all these women from different races and countries came together and were working together. It was all about cooperation. Although *some* women were still petty and jealous, and would steal each other's boyfriends."

At this point, Diva stops and stares pointedly at me.

"Hasn't moved on completely," Darcy amends.

The bell finally rings, and Darcy and I pack up our bags and wait for Aviva to collect all her layers—her scarf, her sweater, her leather jacket. Even in spring, Aviva piles on more clothes than an Ellis Island immigrant.

"Are we going to Derek's party?" Aviva asks as she puts on her sunglasses and follows us out of the classroom. "Eugene's gonna bring the boy binder, and I need help picking out a photogenic prostitute."

"Hunter asked me to go," I say, stopping at my locker.

"*Ooooh,*" Aviva coos. "Is it, like, a *date?*"

"I don't think so," I say.

"What's the deal with you guys?" Darcy asks. "Are you together?"

"I don't think so." I shut my locker, turn around, and sigh. "I don't know what's going on. Hunter's been really weird since I asked him to prom."

"Like, asshole weird?" Darcy says, immediately suspicious.

"No! The opposite. He's weirdly nice. He doesn't make fun of me anymore. And yesterday, when I walked into PMS, he stood up."

"He stood up?"

"Like, he stood up *because* I walked in the room," I say. "Like I was the queen or something."

"Lucky," Darcy says. She thinks everyone should stand when she walks in a room because she's school president.

It's not lucky, though. It's awkward. Hunter has been so polite, timid, and boring. He's acting like Johann! And when I'm in PMS with Hunter and Johann, and Hunter is acting like Johann, and Johann is acting like Johann, everyone is quiet and polite. It's driving me crazy.

"Maybe he's confused about what your status is," Aviva

says. "Does he think you're going to the prom as friends? Some girls ask guys, and then say, 'Let's go *as friends.*'"

"I didn't say we were going as friends." I lower my voice, because we're getting closer to pre-calc, and Hunter is in our class.

"If you didn't mention it either way, maybe he's unclear," Aviva suggests.

"Well, what was I supposed to say? What's the opposite of going as friends? Was I supposed to ask, 'Do you wanna go to the prom . . . as lovers?'"

But I shut up just in time, because Hunter is waiting outside our pre-calc classroom.

"Hey, Kell," he says. "Do you need to copy the homework? I did it last night. All of it."

"You did all the homework?" I ask, as Aviva and Darcy look from me to Hunter, smiling. "But you usually copy *my* homework."

When we all go inside, I pull on Aviva's arm and whisper in her ear, "See? He did his homework! He's definitely being weird."

Derek's parents are letting him have a party because, as of tomorrow, he hasn't had to go to the emergency room in six months, which is a long time for him. The party is in Derek's backyard, which is huge, with a swing set, a tree house, and a deck full of rusty lawn chairs. Derek's backyard is a lot like Derek himself—it's fun, it's messy, and it catches on fire sometimes. Like right now.

"This bonfire is *not* properly contained," Darcy says when we come around the deck and see the big, leaping flames and the smoke.

"Do you know if Derek has a license for this? Or buckets of water? Where is the so-called host?"

Darcy stomps off to find Derek, and soon Aviva leaves me, too.

"There's Eugene with the boy binder," she says excitedly. "Here, hold my scarf."

This isn't a big party like homecoming. Derek just invited people he's friends with—Dave, Damian, and a few other guys, who are fighting over whether or not to put more wood on the fire, and coughing a lot from all the smoke—and a bunch of girls. Pam and Amy took two of the rusted chairs up on the deck and, sitting in them like they're thrones, are whispering to each other about everyone down below. There are junior spandexers on one side of the fire, all texting, and sophomores fighting over a bag of marshmallows, and freshmen at the edge of the woods, hunting for sticks to put the marshmallows on.

Just as I look up at the tree house, Hunter comes out of it. When he sees me, he stops, gripping the sides of the open doorway, and grins. Then he clambers down the wood ladder and jumps off four rungs before the bottom.

"Hey! You're here! I'm glad you're here!"

When Hunter runs up to me, I'm happy that he's not awkward and polite anymore, and I also wonder if he's a little bit drunk. When he hugs me, I think he smells like beer, but I'm not sure.

"How's it going? Did you help make the fire? It's huge!" I say.

"Derek was the one building it up bigger," Hunter says. "And Damian was the one trying to contain it. So it's been kind of a balancing act."

"I think Derek's winning out," I say, watching sparks shoot up from the fire.

"Yeah, it's getting pretty scary over there," Hunter says.

Typical Hunter, he hops up onto the railing of the deck and balances there, swinging his legs. He beckons me closer.

"C'mere," he says. "I'll protect you if the fire gets out of hand."

"Oh, yeah?" I lean on the railing, next to Hunter's legs. "You remember how to stop, drop, and roll?"

"Uh...not really," Hunter says, laughing and shaking his head. His hair is growing out—now it's long enough to fall across his eyebrows but not to cover his eyes. That's the perfect length.

"But we're all good, 'cause Derek's mom is a volunteer firefighter."

"Really?"

"Yeah. Well, she learned so much about putting out

fires from Derek growing up, she just figured she could help out."

"Kelly! Kelly!" Aviva is running across the lawn to me, with Eugene trailing behind her. "I can't decide which one!"

So that's how we end up helping Aviva pick out a male escort. Even Darcy is impressed with Eugene's organization; each profile in the boy binder has two pictures, a head shot and a full-body shot, and lists essential information: age, school, height, weight, extracurriculars, hobbies, and dance ability (which ranges from "occasional *Dance Dance Revolution* participation" to "so good he could back up the Biebs"). Also, the boy binder isn't just the boy binder— Eugene has girls in there, and reminds us all that "Julius is totally cool with same-sex couples at the prom."

"He thinks he's being politically correct," Hunter whispers to me, waving some smoke away from my face. "But he's just trying to make as much money as possible."

"What about this one?" Eugene says, tilting the book toward Aviva. "Great jawline *and* he gets a twenty percent discount at Banana Republic. *Ooh*, or this guy. I love this guy. He's half Filipino and knows how to samba."

"*Ooooh . . .*" Aviva looks intrigued.

"*This* guy is a senior, and he's debating between Cornell and Dartmouth."

"That one's for Darcy!" Aviva says. "What do you think, Darcy? An Ivy guy!"

"I don't need a date!" Darcy protests, crossing her

arms. "I don't even wanna go. I have to, because I'm the president."

"Well, I need a date," Derek says, leaning over our shoulders and looking at the binder. "And I don't want to dance by myself, even though I look good doing it."

Derek stands up and starts dancing, waving his lanky arms over his head and closing his eyes.

"You look ridiculous," Darcy tells him. "Sit down."

She tries to pull him down into a chair, but he starts to run away, and Darcy gets up to chase after him. Aviva is arguing with Eugene over prices—it's $300 to rent one of his escorts, and that doesn't even include the ticket she has to buy for him.

"Shouldn't I get a discount?" Aviva says. "You don't have to pay a guy as much to go out with me as other girls. I mean, I'm fun and I'm hot! Doesn't hotness count for something? It's, like, a job perk."

"Hotness as a perquisite..." Eugene muses. *"Hmm..."*

While Aviva's negotiating and Darcy is chasing Derek up the tree house's ladder, Hunter turns to me and reaches out to wave smoke away from my face.

"You think Darcy's gonna give in?"

I shake my head. "No way."

"Derek can be pretty convincing. Hey, I bet you five bucks she gives in."

"Deal."

We shake on it, Hunter putting that hand I know so well in mine. As I pull my hand away, he says, "I'm at least a better prom date than Derek. I promise you that. I dance way better than him."

"Oh, you can dance?"

"I can dance!" Hunter says. "I can box step, I can shuffle ball change. You'll be impressed with my moves."

"I look forward to that."

"And I'm going to wear a real suit. A real suit, with shoes," Hunter promises, leaning toward me, and I wonder again if he drank before this.

"Oh, with shoes?" I smile. "That's good, if we're gonna be dancing."

"I'm gonna give you that flower thing, and everything. I'm gonna be a good date."

"I know you are," I say. "That's why I asked you."

"That's why you asked me? 'Cause you knew I'd wear shoes?" Hunter doesn't seem drunk when he says this — he seems kind of nervous, like he's covering up some real feeling by joking and he's waiting for my answer.

"That's not exactly why I asked you," I tell him. It's so nice outside, and there's that good bonfire smell, and I start wondering if Hunter will kiss me tonight. *Or should I kiss him?*

"Yee-haw!"

Just then, Derek leaps from the tree house and hits the ground. Hard.

"Oh, Jesus," Eugene says, standing up to see what happened. "I think I heard that *crunch* like when I broke my collarbone."

"The bag of pretzels?" Hunter stands up, too.

"The bag of pretzels," Eugene confirms, nodding.

I have no clue why they're talking about pretzels, but I don't have time to ask, because all of us are running down from the deck and around the fire to get to Derek. Darcy climbs down from the ladder and kneels right in the dirt next to Derek, who's rolling to the side and moaning and pulling his knee up to his chest. She pulls his head into her lap and starts taking his pulse. All of us surrounding them are waiting for Derek to stop moaning and say something. Finally, he does.

"I almost made it six months," he says, and slumps down against Darcy's knees. He grabs his ankle while she takes off his hat and soothingly rubs his head.

"She's a goner," Hunter tells me. "You owe me five bucks."

I smile at him through the smoke. "Oh, I'll pay you back."

He smiles at me, too — this cute smirk that curls one side of his mouth up — and I'm pretty sure we're not going anywhere as friends.

CHAPTER 30: HUNTER

"Escort Etiquette:
A Manners Guide for a Rented Man"

"The Boy Recession©" by Aviva Roth,
The Julius Journal, May

O pen up," Eugene says.

When I open my mouth, Eugene sprays some horrible-tasting breath-spray crap on my tongue. Usually I would complain, spit it out, or accuse Eugene of poisoning me—but not tonight. Tonight I'm on my best behavior. I didn't get pissed when Eugene put gel in my hair. I didn't get pissed when he sprayed me down with cologne. And I let him shut me in his bathroom with his barber, Roberto, to get a straight-razor shave. Tonight, Eugene is the boss of me.

Eugene is also the boss of eleven other dudes. His escort scheme actually turned out to be pretty successful—seven senior girls and five junior girls got dates. Aviva's going with this dude who Eugene has a man-crush on, and Amy's going with this huge blond dude who looks like Peyton Manning if he got punched in the nose. Man, Eugene is going to clean up on this deal tonight. Although I guess he's got a lot of expenses, too. He's got to pay all these guys to be here, and he also rented all the tuxes (he rented mine, too, but I paid him). When I got here, there was this huge rack of suits in Eugene's living room. It took me, like, fifteen minutes to find the one with my name on it.

The prom doesn't start 'til eight, and we don't meet up for pictures 'til seven, so I had no clue why I had to be at Eugene's house at five. But he's got this dude assembly line set up, and he's methodically checking us over and fixing us up—first, he sprayed everyone with cologne and gelled our hair. Then came the breath check, and now he's tying bow ties and putting our pocket squares in our jackets.

"Whoa," Derek says from the couch, where he's stretched out with his cast propped up on cushions. The tree-house leap left him with two broken bones in his ankle. "Watching this is such a trip. Eugene looks like a child laborer in a Ken-doll factory."

When Eugene reaches the end of the line, he says, "Looking good, boys! Everyone go get your corsages out of the fridge. They're labeled. Do not—I repeat, do *not*—take the wrong color. I can't handle any color clashing tonight."

The other escorts file into Eugene's kitchen, but I hang back with Derek and the D-Bags, who are on the couch, watching TV. The D-Bags were not part of the dude assembly line. And you can tell when you look at them, because they kinda look like crap. In Derek's case, it's not his fault. He's got a cast halfway up to his knee, and he's on crutches, so he had to have his mom put his tux on. By the time they figured out what to do with the pants, they were super-wrinkled. He's also wearing his baseball hat, even though Darcy told him not to wear it. Everyone's pretty pumped to see Darcy's face when she sees him.

Dave is wearing a suit, not a tux, and he actually owns it—the thing is, he's owned it since he was thirteen and going to someone's bar mitzvah, and it's too small. Dave is a small dude, but his suit is even smaller, and the pants are too short, so you can see his white socks. This senior girl asked Dave, because she was so desperate for a date she was willing to put up with Dave being mean to her. I guess she didn't have the money for an escort.

Damian's going with one of Maddy Berg's friends who plays *World of Warcraft* with us. They were both online playing at, like, 2 AM one night, and somehow they decided to go to the prom together. Damian rented a tux, but he got one with a white jacket, so he's super pale in this white jacket and black pants, and he looks like a ghost waiter. Derek keeps trying to order drinks from him.

Usually I would be over there on the slacker couch, screwing around with those guys and being a total mess, with pieces of potato chip in my hair and my fly open or whatever. Not tonight. Tonight, I'm not even sitting down; I'm pacing around Eugene's family room because I don't wanna wrinkle my pants.

"Yo, Derek," I say. "Are you guys gonna practice at all?"

But the D-Bags are busy daring one another to eat parts of their corsages. Of course Derek goes first.

"Ew, dude!" he says, laughing and making a face as he moves the piece of leaf around in his mouth with his tongue. "This thing is plastic!"

"You bought Darcy a plastic corsage?" Damian asks. "I don't know if she'll be cool with that."

"Crap. You bought mine, too," Dave says, trying to pull the sleeves of his jacket down. "You are the cheapest bastard. Give me my fifteen bucks back."

"Yo, *Derek*!" I say, walking over to the couch, all official in my nice tux. "Can you guys, like, go rehearse, please?"

Derek looks up at me. "Huh?"

"The thing! My surprise . . . thing! Can you go practice it? The instruments are out in the garage."

"They're in the garage?" Derek says. "How are they getting to the prom place? Because I can't lift shit." He nods at his cast.

"Roberto's driving them over," I say.

"The *barber*?"

"Eugene hired him for the whole night, and he shaved everyone already, so . . ."

The D-Bags mumble and bitch under their breaths, but they give in and head for the garage. As Damian passes me, he claps his hand on my shoulder and says, "Breathe, Hunter. You seem a little uptight."

All the escorts start coming in with their corsages, and Eugene sits them down on the couches in front of the TV.

"All right, boys!" he announces. "We're gonna get a little education in dance-floor etiquette and conversation!"

When the movie comes on, there's a bunch of people from the 1700s or something doing some English version of square dancing while a few dudes play the violin. The guys are in what looks like Revolutionary War gear, with popped collars, and the girls have some push-up-bra action going on.

"Eug, what is this?" I ask him.

"*Pride and Prejudice!*" Eugene says, tossing the DVD remote to one of the guys on the couch and coming back to stand with me. "Girls love this shit. Trust me."

One escort turns around to say, "This version's not bad. But I prefer the BBC miniseries. Six hours. I own it, if you're interested."

When the guy turns back around, Eugene tells me, "I got him from the divorced parents' meeting."

On-screen, the main girl is telling the guy she's dancing with something like, "*It is your turn to say something, Mr. Darcy. I talked about the dance. Now you ought to remark on the size of the room or the number of couples.*"

"Hear that, boys?" Eugene says, smacking one of the guys on the couch on the back of the head. "You gotta be making conversation on the dance floor."

The two guys next to me, buddies who go to Catholic school in Milwaukee together, seem kind of nervous about this whole thing.

"Okay, so first I tell you how big the room is," the first guy says. "Then you tell me how many couples there are."

Eugene turns to me and asks, "You ready to roll, Hun-tro? You got your corsage?"

"Crap," I say. "I forgot something already."

We go into the kitchen, and Eugene opens his fridge, takes out the last corsage, and shows it to me. It's kind of white.

I make a face at it. "Is that right? She said her dress was green."

"It goes with green," Eugene tells me. "Trust me."

Eugene slides my flower thing onto the counter and puts his hand on my shoulder.

"Hunter, relax. I took care of everything. You're good."

"I'm good," I say, looking down. "Shit! My pants got wrinkled! I didn't even sit down!"

"Hunter," Eugene says. "Listen to me. I know you. When you actually give a shit about something, you do a hell of a job at it."

With both hands, he grabs my face.

"Kelly is lucky to have you," Eugene says. "Because you're gonna be a killer date."

I laugh. "Was this a heart-to-heart, dude?"

"Hell, yeah!" Eugene says.

I think Eugene wants me to hug him, but I don't—I just grab my corsage and follow Eugene back into the family room, where the guys are getting pretty into the movie. One of the two nervous guys behind the couch says to the other, "So I think I got it down. He was a real dick in the beginning, but he became less of a dick throughout the night, and then she thought he was a nice guy. So you have to start out the night being a dick, and then get nice."

Eugene turns to me sharply and warns, "Don't listen to that. Don't be a dick."

CHAPTER 31: KELLY

"My Night with a Prom-stitute:
Aviva Roth's True Account of Paying for a Date"

"The Boy Recession©" by Aviva Roth,
The Julius Journal, May

This is as romantic as my prom night is going to get," Darcy says. "Taping Aviva's nipples down."

It's prom night, and we're in the fancy bathroom of the Milwaukee hotel, which has velvet couches and carpet and full-length mirrors. It's pretty glamorous for a bathroom — and we're pretty glamorous for us. Darcy went for a ballerina-chic look, with a black corset dress with a short tulle puffy skirt with her hair slicked back in a tight pony-tail. I'm in a long emerald-green dress, and I got my hair professionally done for the first time. Apparently my hair is so hopeless that they had to straighten it *and* curl it. It seemed counterproductive, but it looks really pretty now. Aviva's gold dress is so low-cut that she can't wear a regular bra with it. She had to wear these sticky chicken-cutlet things instead, which is what we're working on now.

"Your prom night is romantic!" I tell Darcy. "Derek is a fun date. And your corsage is gorgeous!"

Darcy rolls her eyes at the red roses on her wrist.

"*I* bought this," Darcy says. "I bought one for myself because I knew he would disappoint me. He tried to give me a plastic corsage with a bite out of it. Who *bit* my corsage? I can't say for sure—but I'm guessing it was my date. And he wore that stupid hat and ruined all the pictures we took."

"But you guys are so cute, dancing with him on his crutches!" I say. "He's danced with you the whole night, and it can't be easy with a cast on."

Darcy shakes her head, but I can see in the mirror she's trying not to smile.

"Slide it a little bit higher," Aviva tells me. "Okay, perfect! Darcy, gimme the dress tape."

Touching Aviva's boobs isn't the most romantic part of my night. Hunter has been such a great date. He posed for pictures with me, opened doors for me, and pulled out chairs for me. He asked me to dance right away, and he actually leads when we dance.

"Okay, they're stuck to me!" Aviva announces, turning sideways to admire her profile in the mirror.

"Viva, how's the date going?" I ask, sitting on the arm of the fancy couch. "He's *really* cute!"

"He is super-cute," Aviva agrees. "Even up close! And he's a dancing fiend. When that Shakira song came on... his hips did *not* lie. This may be the best three hundred dollars I ever spent. I plan on highly endorsing prostitution in the school newspaper."

I smile at Darcy. "And the student journalism award goes to..."

"Not everyone is so happy, though," Aviva says, stopping to apply lip gloss at the mirror. "Sylvia Sanchez wants a refund. Her date is super-awkward and keeps talking about how big the room is. She thinks he just got out of prison or something."

"No way." I shake my head. "Hunter said Eugene got professional background checks on all the escorts. Maybe he's talking about the room because he wants to be an architect!"

"Okay, let's go," Darcy says, snapping her clutch shut. "I have to announce the prom king and queen."

"*Oooh*, do you know who it is?" Aviva asks.

"Don't know and don't care," Darcy says, pushing the door open. "Bobbi counted the votes."

In the ballroom, the dance floor is almost empty. I go to our table, where Hunter is waiting for me with two pieces of cake.

"Which do you like better?" he asks, standing up to pull out my chair. "Corner piece or middle piece?"

"Whichever one you don't like."

"I eat everything and anything," Hunter says. "You'll learn that about me."

I give in and point to the corner piece, which has more frosting. Hunter slides it over to me and hands me a fork.

"Where's Derek?" Darcy comes up to the table holding two gold envelopes.

"He's doing something," Hunter says, through a mouthful of cake.

"That's not true," Darcy says, rolling her eyes. "Derek is never doing anything."

"Darcy," Hunter says. "He's doing something *important*."

Darcy shuts her mouth and nods. I look from Darcy to Hunter, confused. I'm about to ask what's going on, but Darcy interrupts my thought.

"How do I look?"

I reach out and fluff her tulle skirt. "So cute. Good luck with your announcement!"

Darcy climbs up on the little stage in the front of the room next to the DJ booth, and Hunter and I turn our chairs so we're facing that way. Up at the microphone, Darcy clears her throat.

"Hi, everybody. I'm up here to introduce tonight's prom queen, prom king, and best couple. As I introduce them, please keep in mind that these positions come with no responsibility and zero political clout, and are merely the result of a shallow, antiquated popularity contest...."

Then she opens the envelope casually, to prove that she really doesn't care.

"The Julius P. Heil High School prom queen is...Amy Schiffer," Darcy says with a shrug.

Amy immediately pops up out of her seat, shrieking. She came with one of Eugene's escorts, this very beefy blond guy, and she hugs him before running up onto the stage. At the same table, Pam looks super-bitter, and she tries to get Josh to turn to look at her. But Josh is totally focused on Darcy, and he's already buttoning up his suit jacket. He's sure he's going to be prom king.

"The Julius P. Heil High School prom king is..." Darcy stops and frowns at the envelope. "Um... Scott Paganelli?"

What? Who is Scott Paganelli? I turn to Hunter, but he shrugs, equally clueless. No one is clapping.

"Yay!" Amy shrieks and pushes Darcy out of the way and takes the microphone. "It's my date, Scott! Come up here, Scott!"

At Amy's table, Pam and Josh are looking seriously angry. "He's got a pedigree," Eugene explains to us. "He was king at three Catholic school proms last year. That's how I sold him to Amy."

Darcy gives Amy and Scott their crowns. While Amy is trying to figure out how to put hers on without messing up her already frizzy red curls, Darcy sighs and opens the second envelope.

"The Julius P. Heil High School prom best couple is... Bobbi Novak and Eugene Pluskota."

Around us, everyone is clapping really loudly — they're probably excited to hear two names they actually know. Plus, Eugene's escorts are standing at their respective tables and giving him a standing ovation. I turn around to see how Bobbi is reacting, expecting a squeal at such a high decibel it belongs on a Mariah Carey album. But

Bobbi is very calm. She comes over to our table, smiles at all of us, and extends her hand to Eugene.

Eugene takes her hand and stands up. The applause is really loud, but we're so close that we can hear what he says to her.

"How did this happen?" he asks. "We're not even together anymore! How did people think to vote us best couple?"

Bobbi can't contain herself. Her face is all warm and happy and glowing from the candlelight of our table.

"I rigged it!" she tells him. "I rigged the vote!"

At first Eugene looks surprised, but then he looks touched and proud. And then I think he looks down her dress, but just for half a second. "That's my girl," he says.

A slow song is on, and Scott and Amy are already out on the floor, dancing, and Bobbi and Eugene join them.

For some reason, Darcy is still onstage, even though she opened all her envelopes already, and when the song winds down, she goes to the microphone again.

"And now an announcement I am happy to make," Darcy says. "We welcome to the stage for their debut performance a band that is still searching for an appropriate name but is currently called . . . the D-Bags."

I turn to ask Hunter, "Is Derek really playing?" But Hunter is standing up and buttoning his jacket. *What's going on?*

"This is my cue," he tells me, and before I can say

anything, he jogs to the front of the room, jumps up onto the stage, and pulls back the red curtain. I see Derek — sitting in a chair — and my first thought is that Hunter and Derek are going to pull some prank. But Darcy backs up, handing Hunter the microphone, and I realize that if Darcy's in on this, it can't be a joke.

"So hey, everybody," Hunter says, looking around at all the tables. "Hey, Scott, Amy — congrats, guys. So I'm not actually in the D-Bags; I'm just up here to sing you one song. But I'm a total slacker, as you all know, so it's the same song I sang at the talent show thingy a few months ago. When I wrote the song, I thought that it was about my bed. But I think subconsciously...or unconsciously...I kinda wrote it about someone else, who helped me with the song. She's my date tonight, so...Kelly, this is for you."

Everyone is looking at me.

"You're the healer, I'm the holder...."

Hunter looks so good in his tux, with his hair falling across his forehead, leaning forward into the microphone. And he sounds amazing. And surprisingly, the D-Bags sound pretty good, too.

"You're the soft place that I fall, after all...."

By the second verse, people get up to dance. At my table, Aviva's date is itching to get up and dance some more, so he pulls her out of her seat. On her way to the floor, she squeezes my shoulder.

As the song winds down, I'm the only person left at our table, but I don't mind. When the DJ puts on another slow song, Dave and Damian leave their instruments and come down from the stage. Darcy is waiting for Derek, holding his crutches. Hunter jumps off the stage and comes back to the table.

"How did that happen?" I ask him, in amazement.

Hunter shrugs and laughs.

I stand up to hit him playfully on the lapel of his tuxedo.

"Tell me! Tell me everything!" I beg. "How were you allowed to do that? Since when are the D-Bags actually a *band*? When did they learn your song? Tell me everything!"

Hunter laughs again, and pulls me out onto the dance floor with everyone else. Right away, he takes the lead, pulling me in close, with his hand on the small of my back.

"So?" I ask.

"A lotta people helped out," Hunter says. "Eugene, and Eugene's barber, and..."

"Eugene's barber?"

"I gave the lessons, though," Hunter says. "I mean, the song was easy, but none of those guys ever played an instrument before. We've been practicing, like, every day."

"But Dave was playing the bass!" I say. "You taught him how to play the bass? You know how to play the bass?"

"Kinda, I guess," Hunter admits, shrugging. "Teaching Dave wasn't too bad. Teaching Derek was the worst, 'cause I was scared he was gonna do something to my guitar—like, smash it or something. But he couldn't do anything too bad with the crutches and all."

"I can't believe you taught them!" I say. "In such a short time! What, like, a month?"

"Well, you're the one who said I could teach," Hunter says. "So I guess it all started with you."

Hunter pulls me in really close and kisses me. He smells good, and he feels good, and his sleeves are soft against my arms, and his mouth is soft against my mouth.

We kiss for a long time, and when we finally look up, a lot of people have left the dance floor, which should be embarrassing, but I don't care. "Hey," Hunter says, pointing to our table. "Look."

They're half blocked by Derek's crutches, but Darcy and Derek have turned their chairs toward each other, Darcy is wearing Derek's hat, backward—and they're kissing.

"Maybe I owe you more than five dollars on that bet," I say.

"Nahhh," Hunter says, his arms still around me. "The satisfaction of being right is enough for me."

I laugh.

"So whadda you think?" he asks in his slow, easy voice, smiling down at me. "Am I a good date?"

"You're more romantic than a Taylor Swift song," I tell him.

CHAPTER 32: HUNTER

"Recession Wrap-Up:
What We've Learned and How We Can Grow"

"The Boy Recession©" by Aviva Roth,
The Julius Journal, June

Hey-o!" I call out to Eugene and Derek as I stroll down the dock to Eugene's sailboat.

It's the first day of summer vacation, and there's an awesome wind for sailing. Eugene and Derek are already on the boat, waiting for me.

"You're late!" Eugene tells me as I climb over the side. He's got the boat all ready for sailing. Derek isn't helping at all, but to be fair, he's still got the cast on. "Damn, Huntro," he says, and whistles. "Check you out!"

I'm wearing a polo shirt and khakis. These are the nicest clothes I've had on since prom, which was a month and a half ago.

"Did your girlfriend dress you up?" Eugene asks.

"Nah." I shake my head, hopping up onto one of the side railings. "I had a job interview!"

"What?" Eugene squawks, taking off his sunglasses to examine me. "Seriously?"

"Hell, yeah. And I got the job!"

"What is it?"

"I'm teaching guitar lessons at the music school. I put Derek down as a reference. He told them how I taught him to play guitar in a month and got him his first public gig."

"It's all true," Derek says, sitting up to stretch and accidentally knocking his hat off. "I also told them I was recovering from an injury at the time, so you have experience working with the disabled."

"Well, it worked," I say. "I've got a job."

"First day of summer and you're already employed," Derek says, putting his hat back on. "Pretty impressive, Huntro."

"Actually, it's not that impressive," Eugene contradicts him, stepping over Derek to do something with a rope. "Considering he started job-hunting over a year ago."

"Hey!" I say to Eugene. "Gimme some credit, dude. I'm wearing a shirt with a collar."

"All right. Are we ready to set sail?" he asks.

I hop down from my railing, go sit by Derek, and take out my phone.

"We gotta wait for Kelly," I tell Eugene. "She's on her way. Is Bobbi coming out with us?"

Eugene shakes his head.

"She's away on a retreat."

Derek, who's scratching all around the edge of his cast,

looks up to say, "I thought you guys were going on a retreat next week."

"That's a different retreat," Eugene says, rolling his eyes. "The one she's on now is the Christian teen retreat. The one I have to go to with her is the young Christian couples retreat."

"Well, look at you," I say to Eugene, as I put my foot up on Derek's cast. "Saintly little gingerbread boy."

He tries to whip me with a rope, but he completely fails at it.

Eugene and Bobbi are back together, and Eugene is dealing with the fact that he can't flirt with other girls and that Bobbi still won't let him touch her boobs. Seriously, though, I think he's pretty happy. But Eugene's not the only dude around here with a girlfriend. I've got one, too. I've got a job, a shirt with a collar, and a girlfriend. And this girlfriend is actually *not* a psycho, which is a step up from Diva. Kelly and I have been dating since the prom. We never actually decided to be boyfriend and girlfriend. I just kept asking her to hang out, and we kept hanging out until one day Derek or Eugene or someone referred to her as my girlfriend, and she seemed to be okay with it.

But I have to keep reminding myself she's my girlfriend—like now, as she comes down the dock with Darcy, and she's laughing and the wind is blowing her hair and she looks completely awesome. At times like this, I realize that this whole year and all the crap I had to deal with were all worth it. This year was so ridiculous for me—being in the play, getting that ulcer, learning how to dance, cutting my hair, going to the emergency room, getting yelled at for my grades, getting yelled at for wearing a blue-green shirt instead of a blue shirt. But I guess dealing with all that bullshit got me off my ass so Kelly noticed me.

And now she's actually my girlfriend. She must be, because after I help her onto the boat, she kisses me.

"Congrats on the job!" Kelly says. "That's so exciting! You are going to be an awesome teacher."

Kelly was the first person I called after I got the job. I called her even before I called Derek, and he was my reference.

I help Darcy onto the boat, too, and when she sees Derek lying on the deck, she glares at him.

"I would've helped you!" Derek says. "But I can't stand up!"

"You wouldn't have helped me either way," Darcy says.

"Come here." Derek stretches both arms out to Darcy. "Come here and kiss me, wife."

Derek always tells Darcy that they're gonna get married, but when he says it, Darcy shoots him the same no-chance-in-hell look she's got on her face right now. Derek and Darcy are not dating. But they do actually hook up sometimes. It wasn't just at prom—that was the only time they made out in public, but apparently they've made out a few other times since. Kelly told me that Darcy hooks up with Derek only in dark or sketchy places, the way girls used to hook up with me. Darcy and Kelly sit down on either side of me, and Kelly says, "Eugene, your boat is really nice! When Hunter told me you kept all your beer on a boat, I was kind of picturing a canoe with a few cases of Milwaukee's Second-Best on it."

"Do you have life jackets on here?" Darcy asks.

Kelly turns to me and says in a low voice, "Aviva makes us watch *Titanic* every weekend. It's made Darcy a little paranoid."

"I gave a seminar on nautical safety earlier," Eugene tells Darcy sarcastically. "You missed it because you were *late*."

"Sorry, Eugene," Kelly says. "We were saying good-bye to Aviva. She's leaving for engineering camp."

"Seriously?" I say. "I didn't even know she liked math."

"Oh, she hates it," Kelly says. "But engineering camp is eighty percent guys."

"So she's looking for a dude?" Derek asks.

"No, surprisingly," Darcy says. "She's going under-cover to report on it. She's calling it 'The Girl Recession.' She's gonna be gone for six weeks!"

"Don't worry," Derek says, grabbing on to the railing and pulling himself up. "I'll keep you company when she's away."

He grabs on to the mast and supports himself while he hops over to Darcy. She doesn't help him at all, but when he sits down, she smiles. Derek looks at me and mouths the words *Feelin' the kid.*

Eugene, who's leaning over the side of the boat, untying .

the dock rope and giving us all a nice full view of his ass, turns back to ask, "Everyone ready to set sail?"

For some reason, everyone else looks at me, like I'm the decision-maker or something. Darcy is trying to wrestle a cigarette lighter out of Derek's hand, but they both stop and look up at me. So I shrug, put my arm around Kelly, and give Eugene the signal.

"Let's go for it," I say.

MANY THANKS TO THE FOLLOWING PEOPLE: my agent, Dan Lazar, who handles all the aspects of publishing that I'm clueless about; my editor, Elizabeth Bewley, who worked tirelessly to help me find this story's focus and direction; everyone else at Writers House and Little, Brown; Rachel Markwiese, who gave me the inside scoop on Whitefish Bay; my family and friends, especially the ones who visited me at the library and entertained me on Gchat while I rewrote and revised this manuscript; and all the people whose names I borrowed for characters (with or without permission).

Where stories bloom.

poppy

Visit us online at
www.pickapoppy.com